"It really worked!"

We both start to say at the same time. We stop. Then again, we both speak at once. "One of us has got to let the other one—"

We laugh nervously. "Go ahead. You go first," we both say.

"Okay, I will," the duplicate says quickly. "What are you? Do you know that I just made a copy of myself, and it's you? Do you know who you are, and who I am?"

"You just made a copy of yourself?" I whisper, suddenly feeling very cold.

"I sure did," the duplicate says.

"No." I shake my head. "You got it all wrong. I'm David. I'm the one that's been here all along. I'm the one that made the copy—and you're the copy."

"Nope," says the duplicate, also shaking his head, and sounding very sure of himself. "I'm David; you're the copy."

"This is crazy!" I burst out, scared now but also angry. "Come on, stop playing games. I know I'm the real David."

"Prove it," says the duplicate.

—⚏—

William Sleator is the author of many acclaimed novels, including the best-selling *Interstellar Pig* and *Singularity*. His most recent novel is *The Boxes*.

He says, "My brother Danny, a computer scientist, gave me the idea for this book. I thought it was a very funny idea. But when I sat down and brainstormed, trying to be completely logical about it, I came up with a book that was totally different from what I had first imagined. There are certain passages that still make me scream."

Mr. Sleator divides his time between Boston and Bangkok, Thailand.

PUFFIN BOOKS BY WILLIAM SLEATOR

WILLIAM SLEATOR
THE DUPLICATE

PUFFIN BOOKS

PUFFIN BOOKS
Published by the Penguin Group
Penguin Putnam Books for Young Readers,
345 Hudson Street, New York, New York 10014, U.S.A.
Penguin Books Ltd, 27 Wrights Lane, London W8 5TZ, England
Penguin Books Australia Ltd, Ringwood, Victoria, Australia
Penguin Books Canada Ltd, 10 Alcorn Avenue, Toronto, Ontario, Canada M4V 3B2
Penguin Books (N.Z.) Ltd, 182-190 Wairau Road, Auckland 10, New Zealand

Penguin Books Ltd, Registered Offices: Harmondsworth, Middlesex, England

First published in the United States of America by E. P. Dutton,
a division of NAL Penguin Inc., 1988
Published by Puffin Books,
a member of Penguin Putnam Books for Young Readers, 1999

10 9 8

THE LIBRARY OF CONGRESS HAS CATALOGED THE DUTTON EDITION AS FOLLOWS:
Sleator, William.
The duplicate / William Sleator.—1st ed.
    p. cm.
Summary: Sixteen-year-old David, finding a strange machine that creates
replicas of living organisms, duplicates himself and suffers the horrible consequences
when the duplicate turns against him.
ISBN 0-525-44390-8 (hc.)
[1. Science Fiction.] I. Title.
PZ7.S6313Du 1988 [Fic]—dc19 87-30562 CIP AC

Puffin Books ISBN 0-14-130431-6

Printed in the United States of America

This book is for Ann Durell,
as all of them really are.

What am I going to do about Angela?

"Where are you going, David?" Mom asks me as I'm on my way out the back door.

"Down to the beach to see if anything got washed up by the storm." It's partly true. I don't stop to look at her, pulling on my jacket.

"Well, don't forget we're having supper at Grandma's tonight," she calls after me. "You'd better be back by five to get cleaned up."

"Okay." I push the door shut behind me and take the steps two at a time. It's an overcast day in October with a chilly wind, perfect weather for the mood I'm in. We live a quarter of a mile from the beach, and I walk quickly, trampling through the leaves on the sidewalks, kicking aside the small tree limbs that were blown down by the storm last night, trying to think of a solution.

I remember how excited I was on Friday when I finally made a date with Angela. She told me she didn't understand the math assignment. "Well," I said, and I *think* I sounded pretty casual about it, "how about if I just drop over sometime over the weekend and explain it to you?"

"Great," she said, not hesitating for a second, shaking back her crinkly red hair. "I'm going away for the weekend with my family, but we'll be back Sunday afternoon. You can eat over. We'll get the math over with fast and then do something fun."

"What about Carl?" I said, before thinking better of it.

"What about him?" she said, shrugging.

"Nothing," I said. We both laughed.

I've been thinking about Angela a lot since the beginning of the school year. I've even had dreams about her. She's extremely good-looking and a very enthusiastic type of person. The only reason I haven't asked her out before this is that I know she's been going out with Carl. He's sort of a snotty jerk—I sit next to him in band. I wonder how he'll feel about me going over there. But if she doesn't think he's a problem, why should I? I'm really crazy about her.

Anyway it doesn't matter anymore, because I stupidly forgot about my grandmother's dumb birthday party. I can't even tell Angela until the last minute because she won't be back until late this afternoon. I mentioned to my parents, several times, that I have a lot of homework and might not be able to go to my grandmother's. They told me to get the homework done before Sunday night. They won't believe me if I pretend to be sick. But if I cancel out on Angela when she's depending on me, just to go to my *grandmother's*, she'll probably think I'm a jerk. No matter what I do, somebody will be mad at me. And it's all my own fault.

2

The same thing has happened to me before. I forget I'm supposed to do something dull, and make another commitment to do something fun, and then I'm forced to let somebody down. But I can't stand to have that happen with Angela!

Still, as much as I don't want to, I know I'll end up going to my grandmother's. I'm a good son, decent, well behaved, and all that boring stuff.

The beach is deserted today because of the lousy weather. As I get closer to the surf, I find more and more satisfyingly disgusting things washed up by the storm—tentacles of seaweed embracing pulpy jellyfish; lots of dead fish, already stinking; a couple of sea gulls with broken necks. I poke through the debris with a long piece of driftwood, pushing things aside, turning small rocks over to see what's underneath. I no longer really expect to find a bottle with a message in it, but I still keep trying.

I'm sixteen, and for as long as I can remember, I always seem to end up at the beach when I don't know what else to do. I feel more comfortable here than in my own backyard, as though the beach belongs to me somehow. I'm whistling some tune I don't even recognize, thinking how great it would be if I really could go over to Angela's tonight.

I notice a very strange object, tangled in a mass of seaweed, which seems to be charred, weirdly enough. Maybe the thing was hit by a bolt of lightning during the storm, after it was washed up on the beach. I push the seaweed away from the object with the stick and squat down to look at it.

It's even more peculiar, on closer examination, than I realized at first. I've never seen anything like it. It looks

3

like a combination postage scale and video camera. There's a small platform at one side, or maybe it's a lever, because it looks as though it might move if you pushed down on it. Next to the platform is a hollow tube, like a vacuum cleaner tube, that feeds into the central portion, an oddly shaped box. A kind of lens pokes out of the box, just above the tube. The whole thing is about the size of a portable television.

I look closer. From a certain angle I can see silvery letters across the top of the box, strangely shaped. It's hard to make them out, but what they seem to be saying is *Spee-Dee-Dupe*.

"Spee-Dee-Dupe? What's that supposed to mean?" I say to myself. I stand up and back away, to look at it from a distance and see if that will give me a better perspective on it. Could it be something that fell out of a boat or an airplane?

A sea gull, attracted by a dead fish nearby, flaps and struts toward the object. It's not particularly afraid of me; people are always feeding the gulls on this beach. The bird stops beside the lever. It twists its neck and spreads its feathers. It stretches its head forward and rests its beak on the platform at the end of the lever. I wonder if I should scare the gull away from it, but don't. The bird pushes down on the platform, and the lever moves.

There's a dull pop and a bright flash of light from the lens. I cry out in surprise, and blink. There are two sea gulls standing beside the lever.

"Huh? Where'd the other one come from so fast?" I whisper. I didn't notice the second gull approaching. It must have fluttered down in the instant I blinked. The two birds study each other for a moment, then hop off together toward the dead fish. Their scrawny legs move exactly in step with one another, like two soldiers marching. They look absolutely identical—but then all sea gulls look alike, don't they?

Still, it's very odd the way the second gull appeared so quickly. I could swear it just burst into existence out of nowhere, except I know that's impossible. But why didn't I see it coming, then? I look over at the gulls. They both have the same piece of fish in their beaks now, fighting over it, tugging it back and forth. They seem to be equally strong; neither one can get the fish away from the other.

Spee-Dee-Dupe. What could it mean? The first part is obvious: speedy. If the object actually did anything, it did it fast. But what about *Dupe*?

I have an idea.

It's crazy, it's too fantastic to be real. But why can't I test it out? I look at the two sea gulls again. They're fighting more violently now. I walk back to the object and touch the box part of it with one finger. It feels just like ordinary plastic. I pick it up, being very careful not to touch the platform or the lever. It's no heavier than an ordinary radio. I quickly carry it home.

5

2

I get it up to my room without anyone else noticing it, set it carefully down on the floor, and close the door. If the fantastic idea I have about it is true—and I hardly dare to believe that it might be—then it has to be some kind of top secret device. Or else it's an artifact from the future, or another planet or something, that was somehow carried here by the storm. But that really is crazy. I can't start thinking like that.

I'm dying to test it, and I don't have a lot of time. I look around quickly for a convenient object and take a felt-tipped pen from my desk. I sit down beside the Spee-Dee-Dupe. Making sure that no part of my finger is anywhere near its surface, I touch the end of the pen to the platform and push down. The lever moves.

There is no dull pop, no flash of light, nothing. And there's still only one pen in my hand.

"Shoot!" I knew it probably wouldn't work, but I'm still really disappointed. I guess I just didn't notice that second gull approaching.

But why was there no pop this time, and no flash? I try again with the pen, pressing harder. Nothing happens. I try it with a pencil, with no result. I try it with the desk clock, and again produce nothing. I get a dollar bill out of my wallet, drop it onto the platform, and press down on it with the pen. There is still only one dollar bill.

I know the sea gull didn't do anything more than I'm doing. So why can't I get it to react in any way? I should probably give up now, and face the fact that there's nothing special about the device. But I don't *want* to give up and face facts. I look vaguely around the room, thinking it over, trying to figure out why the sea gull was different from the pen and the clock and the money. I glance over at the aquarium and the one lonely yellow and blue tropical fish swimming there. Then I have another idea.

It takes me a while to get my hand on the fish, which naturally keeps darting away from me. When I do get a hold on it, it slips easily out of my fingers. I try with both hands, not worrying about how wet my shirt is getting. At last I get the thrashing little thing cupped in my two palms. I rush back to the Spee-Dee-Dupe, knowing that the fish can't survive very long out of the water. I drop the fish onto the platform. It slithers off and falls on the floor. I grab it again, set it carefully onto the platform, and push down against the fish with the pen.

The lever moves. There is a dull pop and a bright flash. Two identical yellow and blue tropical fish fall off the platform and writhe miserably on the floor.

I scoop them up and drop them into the aquarium. Excited now, my heart racing, I study the two fish. Their markings are exactly alike in every detail. They swim stupidly around, unaware of what has happened, not yet

7

paying any attention to each other. But, remembering the gulls, I sprinkle more food into the water so that there will be plenty for both of them and they won't have to fight.

It worked, it really did work! It's almost too fantastic to believe—except that I saw the impossible thing happen twice. Apparently the Spee-Dee-Dupe—which has to mean Duplicator—only makes copies of living organisms. That's why nothing happened with the things from my desk, and the money. It's too bad, in a way, that I won't be able to make endless copies of twenty-dollar bills. But what I *can* do is a lot more exciting than that.

Am I really going to do it?

The telephone rings. I get up, sighing, and pick up the receiver. It's Angela. I stop sighing. "We just got back," she says. "What time are you coming over? The sooner the better. We're ordering out for pizza. We can get the math out of the way fast, so we'll have time for some good stuff." She sounds breathless with excitement. It's just like her to phone me without worrying whether or not it's appropriate, without trying to play it cool. When Angela feels like doing something, she does it. "So what time can you come?" she wants to know.

I'm still trying to think logically. After I make a duplicate of myself, will I be able to sneak out of the house and over to Angela's right away, or will I have to wait until the rest of them leave for my grandmother's? I'm not sure. "Well," I say, "Um . . . I guess . . ."

"Come over now," Angela urges me. I think of her red hair. "Your folks know you're eating here, so why shouldn't you come now? Anyway, I want to tell you what we did in the city. Come on."

8

"I'll be right over," I say.

"Great. We'll have so much *fun!* See you soon," says Angela, and hangs up.

I dive for the Spee-Dee-Dupe and slam my hand down on the lever.

Nothing happens.

"*Now* what?" I groan. I can't tolerate any more delays. I press the lever down again, and a third time. Still nothing happens.

Is it possible that it doesn't make copies of human beings, only animals? But that doesn't make sense; human beings are animals too. So what's the problem? I think about the sea gull and the fish, trying to figure out what I'm doing differently this time.

It doesn't take me long to come up with a possible explanation. The Spee-Dee-Dupe only makes copies of living things. And unlike the sea gull and the fish, I'm almost completely covered with nonliving objects. My clothes might be getting in the way, preventing the machine from doing its work. It makes a certain kind of sense. I lock the door and quickly pull off my clothes, letting them drop onto the floor. I sit down again and push the lever with my hand.

I feel a very slight sensation against my skin, like a pin prick. There is a dull pop and a very bright flash. I close my eyes.

3

I open my eyes. Another boy, who looks exactly like me, is sitting beside me on the floor.

"I don't believe it," I whisper, watching the other frightened boy whispering exactly the same words. We both scramble away from each other, our eyes locked together.

"It really worked—" we both start to say at the same time. We stop. Then again, we both speak at once. "One of us has got to let the other one—"

We laugh nervously. "Go ahead. You go first," we both say.

"Okay, I will," the duplicate says quickly. "What are you? Do you know that I just made a copy of myself, and it's you? Do you know who you are, and who I am?"

"*You* just made a copy of yourself?" I whisper, suddenly feeling very cold.

"I sure did," the duplicate says.

"No." I shake my head. "You got it all wrong. *I'm*

10

David. I'm the one that's been here all along. I'm the one that made the copy—and you're the copy."

"Nope," says the duplicate, also shaking his head, and sounding very sure of himself. "I'm David; you're the copy."

"This is crazy!" I burst out, scared now but also angry. "Come on, stop playing games. I *know* I'm the real David."

"Prove it," says the duplicate, who seems to have an annoyingly stubborn personality.

"I just know it, that's all," I insist. "I was here by myself a minute ago. I tested out this thing with the fish. Then Angela called. I figured out I had to take my clothes off, and pressed down on the lever, and after that you were here. I remember everything."

"I remember everything, too," the duplicate says very quietly, sounding just as scared as I am now. We're still staring at each other.

"Well," I say after a moment, shrugging uncomfortably. "I guess . . . in a way, it makes sense. The duplicate seems to come with a complete memory—the Spee-Dee-Dupe must duplicate all the brain cells and everything. So we both think we're the original."

"That's got to be it," the duplicate says.

"Except I know I'm the original," I put in quickly.

"Look, there's no point in arguing about it forever; we'll never agree," says the duplicate. "We just have to accept the fact that we both think we're the original. Okay?"

That's exactly the kind of remark I would make—it's eerie how similar the duplicate's personality is. "You're right," I agree with him. "Let's stop arguing about it."

"Good," the duplicate says. "Now we can move on to

something else—like trying to decide who gets to go to Angela's and who has to go to Grandma's."

"I'm going to Angela's," I say, without thinking.

"Who says you are? I'm the original—I mean, we both have the same memories. We both want to go." He stands up. His body looks pretty good. Is that what my body looks like, or is his better than mine? "The first thing we have to do is put on some clean clothes," the duplicate says. He opens the closet—just as if it's his own closet—and turns and asks me, "Anything you particularly want to wear tonight?"

"Well, I was sort of thinking of wearing that blue shirt over to Angela's," I tell him. I'm not sure I like the idea of sharing my clothes with this other person.

"Who says you're the one who's going over to Angela's?" the duplicate asks me. "We haven't decided that yet."

"But *I'm* the one she invited. I mean . . ." Now I'm confused and annoyed again. I had assumed that I, as the original, would be the one to decide which of us did what. But since the duplicate has this powerful delusion that he's the original, it's not going to be that simple. "Oh, just wear anything you want," I tell him. Deciding what clothes to wear is going to be the least of our problems.

The duplicate leaves the blue shirt in the closet for me. It's a hopeful sign. Maybe my first impression was wrong and the duplicate isn't going to be so hard to get along with after all.

We don't talk while we're putting my clothes on. Then when we're dressed, we both start to say, "Well, I was thinking that the best—"

12

We stop and wait. Then I say, "You were going to say we should flip a coin, right?"

"Right. It's interesting how much we think alike," the duplicate says, reaching into the dirty pants I dropped on the floor, which still have my wallet and change in them. "It's almost like having ESP."

"Not really," I say, fighting the impulse to tell him to keep away from my money. "I mean I can guess what you're going to say because I know you think like me. But I can't actually *hear* your thoughts or anything."

"I can't hear yours, either," the duplicate says, my change in his hand. "Uh . . . I guess we should probably each take half the money." I can tell, by the way he says it, that the guy thinks he's being very generous to offer to share my money with me. I resent it. But getting mad at him won't do any good. He'll still think he's the original—that's the way the device constructed him.

"Okay, we split the money," I agree, feeling generous myself for being so reasonable about it. "But one of us is going to have to get another wallet. We should both chip in for it."

"No problem," the duplicate says. "But whoever goes to Angela's tonight should be the one to keep this wallet—the other one won't need it at Grandma's."

"Fine," I say. I still believe I'll be the one who gets to go to Angela's just because it only seems fair. I reach out my hand. "Here. Give me my half of the money. Then I'll flip."

"Wait a minute. How can I be sure you're not going to cheat?"

"How can I cheat flipping a coin?" I ask, trying to sound

13

reasonable, though I've been worrying about exactly the same thing.

"I don't know," the duplicate says, handing me some money. I count it carefully, it's $5.37, but that doesn't prove he isn't cheating me, since I don't remember how much I had. The only way I can find out is to ask to see how much money he's kept, but that seems cheap.

"I guess it's okay if you flip," I tell him.

"Okay," the duplicate says, and grins at me. I wish I'd kept my mouth shut—I'm always wishing that, after it's too late. The duplicate holds up a dime. "You want to call it in the air?"

"Yeah, yeah, I'll call it in the air," I say, letting my irritation show in my voice.

The duplicate tosses the coin, and I call, "Heads," my eyes fixed on the tumbling dime. It lands in the duplicate's palm, and he flips it over onto his other wrist.

"Tails," the duplicate says, his eyes moving up from the coin to meet mine. I can see the effort he's making to keep his face expressionless and not to look smug. It's infuriating.

"Not fair!" I say.

"What's not fair about it? I just flipped it. You saw the whole thing."

"Yeah, but we never said you would turn it over after it landed," I protest, knowing I don't have much of an argument.

"But that's how you always do it, isn't it?"

"Okay, *you* go to Angela's." I turn angrily away from him. This isn't working out at all the way I imagined it. I never would have made the duplicate if I'd known it was going to be like this.

14

"Oh, come on, don't be mad at me," the duplicate says. "Don't be upset. You don't really think it was unfair, do you?" He seems genuinely concerned.

"Oh, I guess not."

"The main thing is, we've got to try to get along with each other," the duplicate goes on. "If we don't, nothing will work out."

"You're right, I guess." I turn back to face him.

"And next time . . . *you* get to do the fun thing, okay?" the duplicate offers, smiling at me.

"Okay. I'll go along with that," I say, thinking, again, that he might not be too hard to get along with.

Someone knocks on the door. "David, are you talking to yourself?" Mom calls, from out in the hall.

We look at each other, and giggle, and both start to answer at once. The duplicate politely lets me say it. "Yeah, Mom, I guess I was." We giggle again.

"Well, it's time to start getting ready."

I nod at the duplicate to let him know it's his turn to answer.

"Okay, I'm getting cleaned up right now," the duplicate tells her.

We hide the Spee-Dee-Dupe under the bed. A few minutes later, I check out the rest of the house. Mom and Dad are both in their room, changing.

I hurry back to my room. "Okay, the coast is clear, get going," I tell the duplicate. "And . . . have a good time."

"You too," the duplicate says, pausing at the bedroom door. "And remember . . . next time, *you* get to do the fun thing," he repeats, as if he feels a little guilty.

"Fine. Now get going while you have the chance."

The duplicate hurries quietly downstairs. From my window, I watch "myself" leave the house and head off in the direction of Angela's, envying him. We agreed that we will both have to tell each other absolutely everything that happens, so that the next time I'm with Angela, or the duplicate is with Mom and Dad, neither will make any mistakes. Still, I'm not sure how much I can trust the duplicate.

And I ask myself, if I were the one who was going to Angela's, would I come back and tell the duplicate everything that happened—absolutely everything?

I have to admit that I might not.

4

It is very boring at my grandmother's. All I can think about is what they're doing at Angela's. I begin to worry about what will happen if the duplicate gets home later than my parents and I do. We didn't discuss it, but it's a definite possibility, since my grandmother always goes to bed early. At least we were smart enough to make sure that the duplicate had the house key. Still, it would be difficult for the duplicate to try to sneak in with my parents sitting around in the living room. Even if he waits until Mom and Dad are in bed, they might still hear him and think someone's breaking into the house. I can only hope that, since the duplicate's mind is identical to mine, he'll be aware of the problem and make sure to get home first.

It's ten o'clock when I get back to my room. The duplicate isn't there.

Now what am I going to do? Why didn't the duplicate realize how much trouble this could get us into? I pace in the center of the room, trying to think logically, trying not to blame the duplicate too much. I know it would be difficult for him to get away if they were in the middle of a game or a movie, or something else. I might have done the same thing myself if I was having a good time, which the duplicate obviously is. And I resent him for it. The more I think about him and Angela together, the more jealous I get. I know I'm only making everything worse by feeling this way, but I just can't control it.

However selfish and irresponsible the duplicate is, I still have to figure out how to get him inside unnoticed, just for my own sake. After brooding about it for fifteen minutes and coming up with nothing, I decide that the best thing to do is to meet him outside. Maybe the two of us together can come up with something.

My parents are in the living room, watching television. I start down the stairs, not making any attempt to be quiet about it. On the landing, I open my mouth to call out to them that I'm going outside for a few minutes.

I hear the sound of the key turning in the lock, and see the front door begin to open. Just in time, I turn and move quietly back up the stairs.

"David, you startled me!" I hear Mom say. "How did you get outside? I thought you were up in your room."

"Oh. I, uh, just wanted a breath of air," the duplicate says, his voice moving quickly toward the bottom of the stairs. "Good night."

"Wait a minute. Why are you in such a hurry?" The volume of the television goes down. "And why did you change your clothes at this time of night?"

I hold my breath, waiting for the duplicate to come up with an answer.

"Oh, uh, well . . . I spilled some water on that other shirt," the duplicate begins. "And then I wanted to go outside, so I had to . . ."

I don't get a chance to hear the rest of his answer because at that moment I hear a door opening behind me in the second floor hallway. I spin around on the stairs. It's Dad, coming out of his study. He's not downstairs after all. I hurry up, not knowing what else to do.

"Nothing good on TV?" Dad asks me, moving toward the stairs.

"No, I, uh, just came in from a walk," I manage to say. At all costs, I've got to keep Dad from going downstairs, and somehow get him out of the way, until the duplicate is safely hidden in my room. "But Dad," I say, "there was something I wanted to ask you, right away."

"Shoot," Dad says, at the top of the stairs now.

"Well, but could we just go into your study for a minute?" I'm talking loud, so he won't hear the duplicate's voice downstairs. "Come on, just for a minute, okay?" I urge him. It's all I can do not to grab his arm and drag him across the hall.

"Hey, this sounds serious," Dad says, finally moving after me. In the study, I quickly shut the door behind me. "What's on your mind, son?" Dad asks, looking a little worried now. "I thought you seemed preoccupied tonight. Is anything wrong?"

What am I going to say? I have to keep talking so Dad won't hear the duplicate coming upstairs. At the same time, I have to hear the duplicate myself so I'll know when it's safe to let Dad out of the room. "Well, yes, I was kind of wondering about something," I tell him, thinking

19

fast. Dad works for a genetic engineering firm; maybe I can get him started on some subject related to that. "Do you think that they ever really will be able to make living clones of human beings?"

"Huh? *That's* what you were worrying about all evening?" Dad says, sounding skeptical.

"Yes, that's what I was thinking about," I assure him, nodding eagerly. "I was just wondering about what it would be like to have a clone of myself, and whether I would like it or not."

"Couldn't we discuss this some other time?" Dad says. "I thought you had something urgent on your mind."

"Oh, but it *is* urgent," I insist, feeling ridiculous. "I mean, we were supposed to be thinking about it for school tomorrow. We have to write about it in class. So, do you think it would ever be possible to make a clone of a person?"

"Certainly. They've done it with frogs; no reason they shouldn't be able to do it with people. The real question is whether scientists will ever be allowed to do experiments in that area. It's very controversial, of course."

"Yes, go on, Dad," I say, listening for footsteps in the hallway and not paying much attention to what Dad is telling me. "You really do think they could make a copy of a person?"

"Well, yes. But you know it wouldn't be like having a copy of yourself, like a twin. It would be more like having a child. If they took one of your cells and started it growing tomorrow, for instance, the clone would be about seventeen years younger than you. There's no technology that would ever be able to reproduce a person instantly." Dad turns toward the door.

I hear footsteps on the stairs. "Are you *sure* there won't be a method someday to do that?" I ask him.

"Not based even remotely on anything we know today." He opens the door and steps out into the hall before I can stop him. Terrified, I peer out behind him.

The hall is empty. The duplicate must have made it into my room just in time. "Funny," Dad says. "I could have sworn I heard somebody walking out here."

"No, Dad, nobody was here," I say as I back toward the door of my room, speaking loudly so the duplicate will know I'm coming and will get out of sight. "Well, thanks for all the help." I open the door as little as possible and back inside, Dad still watching me, and then push the door closed. I turn and start to say something to the duplicate, who is standing in the far corner of the room, out of sight from the hallway. The duplicate quickly puts his finger up to his mouth. We can't talk until Dad goes downstairs.

It was a close call; I was scared. I'm also angry. The duplicate is to blame for this near disaster, for not getting home first, and I'm impatient to tell him so. It's frustrating to stand there, staring at the duplicate, and not be able to say anything. To distract myself, I walk over to the aquarium.

The two identical fish have finally become aware of each other. They float near the surface, face to face, a few inches apart, slowly opening and closing their mouths. For the first time, I notice that the fish have very sharp little teeth. Which is the original and which is the duplicate? There is, of course, no way of knowing.

Faintly, I hear Dad say something to Mom downstairs. The volume of the television goes up. I turn back to the duplicate. "Why didn't you get home first?" I demand, whispering. "They almost caught us. They could still figure out something's going on, if they talk about it."

"Sorry," the duplicate says, sounding sheepish, his eyes not meeting mine. "It was hard to get away. Angela was so—uh, I mean, we were . . . having fun."

It's not the wisest thing he could say, given the mood I'm in. "Well, that's just great!" I snap at him. "I'm so happy to hear it. We wouldn't want to let keeping our secret from Mom and Dad interfere with a little fun."

"You would have done the same thing yourself," the duplicate says, looking directly at me now.

It might be true, but I'm not going to admit it. "No, I wouldn't. I was worried all night about when you'd get home. I was hoping you'd think about it too. Why didn't you?"

"I *did*," the duplicate insists, thrusting his head forward for emphasis, just as I would have done. "But it would have looked funny to leave right in the middle of—of a game. I even lost on purpose, just to get out of there as soon as I could."

"How noble of you," I say. "You should have told her from the beginning that you had to be home before ten. You could have made up some reason. It *is* a school night."

"Look, I said I was sorry." The duplicate sits down on the bed next to the window—the one I always sleep in. "We didn't get caught, did we? And we learned something. Next time we'll just have to plan more carefully, that's all."

"Yeah, we learned something," I say. "But we could have learned it *without* almost ruining everything."

22

"So I'll be more careful next time," the duplicate says, sighing. "It's not going to help anything if you keep bugging me about it."

"Okay, okay." I'm impatient. "So what happened at Angela's? We have to tell each other everything, from beginning to end."

"Well, first we worked on the math," the duplicate begins. "Then we had pizza. Then—"

"Hold it," I interrupt him. "You know that's not good enough. I need details. Where was Angela when you got there? Which problems did she have trouble with? What kind of pizza? What did you talk about at supper? Anything could be important if Angela says something about it to me tomorrow." I was thinking a lot about this issue of details at my grandmother's, since it was so dull there. I'm surprised that the duplicate has to be prompted this way. "Are you hiding something from me?" I ask him.

"No, no," the duplicate says quickly. "I guess I just wasn't thinking. I'm sort of distracted—it was such a *great* evening."

"Then tell me about it—and don't skip anything."

The duplicate talks. I concentrate hard, trying to remember all of it, repeating certain things that seem important, coming up with more questions. I keep wondering what the duplicate might be leaving out. "What was Angela wearing?" I ask at one point.

"Oh . . . nothing special, jeans and a sweat shirt. Purple, I think. But she sure looked wonderful." And the duplicate smiles to himself, his eyes looking through me as though I'm not there.

I can't stand the expression on his face. "I hope you

didn't stare at her like that. She'd think you were a sap."

The duplicate looks startled. I'm a little surprised at myself too, because I'm not usually nasty.

"Were you ever alone with her?" I ask him.

"No," the duplicate says instantly, looking away from me.

"You better not be lying to me," I say. "You sound funny. You *were* alone with her, weren't you."

"Oh . . . well, yes, for a few minutes," the duplicate reluctantly admits.

"Well? What happened?"

"Nothing," he insists. "I *said* it was only for a little while. Are you going deaf or something?"

Now I'm surprised at *his* nastiness; this situation is making us both hostile. The duplicate's attitude seems to imply that I'm prying—and I do feel uncomfortable about pestering him for all the particulars. But logically I know I'm not prying. I *have* to find out everything, so I won't blunder the next time I see her. "What do you mean, nothing? I know you didn't just sit there in silence. You must have done *something*."

"We talked about . . . school."

"School?" I don't believe him. "Is that all?"

"Yes," the duplicate says, bristling with self-right-eousness. "Angela has Strauss for English. Apparently she makes them write little one paragraph 'observations' every day. Angela has trouble thinking them up. I told her just to make them real sensitive and cornball, like about not killing insects and helping birds with broken wings and things, and she'd get a good grade. All teachers like that kind of phony, *warmhearted* stuff."

24

I wonder if *I* usually sound that cynical. "Was she impressed by that?"

"I don't know," the duplicate says evasively. "I don't know her well enough to tell if she's impressed or not. You know that."

"Well, you must know her a little better after tonight. Did she say anything about Carl?"

"Oh, yeah. She said they're not going steady, and she can do whatever she wants."

"That's all she said about him?"

"Uh-huh," the duplicate says, his eyes wandering vaguely away from me.

I sigh. I can't get rid of the feeling that the duplicate is hiding something. But maybe I'm just being paranoid.

"Well, is the cross-examination over yet?" he asks me.

"I guess so. Don't you want to know what happened at Grandma's?"

"Sure," he says, yawning.

I don't have as much to tell the duplicate about my evening, of course, but I try to be as thorough as possible, giving him all the details. The duplicate doesn't seem to be listening as closely as I think he should. "What's the matter, am I boring you?" I ask him.

"Well, yes, to be honest about it."

"That's tough," I say, a little insulted. "Come on, think. What did Grandma say about Aunt Louise?"

"Huh? Aunt Louise?" The duplicate shrugs, as though it's a stupid question. "*I* don't know."

"I just *told* you one second ago," I say, irritated again. "Why aren't you listening? Aunt Louise changed her will again. Now she's leaving all her money to her cats. Come

25

on, you're not trying. What if Mom says something about it to you tomorrow?"

"What if she does? Isn't that the kind of thing I might have forgotten, even if I *had* been there?"

"Oh." I hadn't thought of that.

"I mean, we've got to be practical about this," the duplicate says. "First of all, we're never going to be able to remember every tiny little thing. If we try to do that, we'll forget what's important. So we should just concentrate on the incidents that count. And anyway, it will look suspicious if we remember *too* much. I forget things like that all the time."

"I guess you're right," I admit.

"It's the same with Angela," the duplicate says. "You keep badgering me to tell you everything she said to me the whole evening. As if you think I'm hiding something. Well, I just don't remember everything she said to me, that's all. And neither would you, if you'd been there." He sits back and crosses his arms, as if he has scored an important point. "Come on, finish up with Grandma's. I'm getting sleepy. It was a big night for me."

I have trouble getting to sleep. I lie in the dark listening to the duplicate in the other bed. I feel afraid of him, in some way I can't explain. To distract myself, I go over everything the duplicate has told me about what happened at Angela's, trying to fix the events in my mind. I wish the duplicate had told me more. But he's probably right about too many little details crowding out the important ones. It's true that I usually don't remember everything.

And yet, somehow, I still don't really trust the duplicate—especially when it comes to Angela.

26

5

It's only about a minute after I wake up that I hear the duplicate whisper, "You awake?"

"Yeah." I turn and look over at the other bed, yawning.

The duplicate is watching me. I can't believe I ever looked as angelic as he does; there is something too sweet about his smile. "I was just trying to make plans," he says. "Since I was the one who got to go over to Angela's last night, I think you should be the one who gets to skip school today, and do anything you want. Okay?"

"Huh?" I say, surprised. I've been looking forward to seeing Angela at school today, and don't like the duplicate's suggestion.

"It only seems fair," the duplicate goes on, with that saintly smile. "Last night you did the boring thing. Today you should do the fun—"

"You think I'm going to fall for that?" I interrupt him, sitting up abruptly.

"Fall for what?" the duplicate says. He sits up too,

looking genuinely puzzled. "I don't know what you mean."

"What I mean," I say heatedly, "is that last night you got to do what *you* wanted. So today, I get to do what *I* want. And what I want is to go to school."

"Okay, okay, you don't have to bite my head off," the duplicate says. "I was just trying to be decent. It's not my fault you didn't sleep well."

"How do you know I didn't sleep well?" I ask him.

"I can just tell by looking at you. And I didn't sleep well either."

I study the duplicate. He looks exceptionally well rested, his eyes bright and alert, his complexion fresh. "You don't look tired to me."

The duplicate sighs and rolls his eyes. "What is it with you? First thing in the morning, and already you're trying to start a fight. That's not like me at all. It makes me wonder if the Spee-Dee-Dupe fried some of your brain cells when it copied me."

"It copied *me*," I can't keep from saying, though I know it's a pointless argument. We stare at each other. Then the duplicate starts to giggle, and in a moment, I'm giggling too, though I don't really know why. "I didn't mean to be nasty," I say. "I really didn't sleep well. And I was just assuming that I would go to school today."

"Listen, if you want to go to school, that's fine with me," the duplicate says, as if he means it. He looks out the window. "Seems like a nice day. I can go back to the beach." He gives me a sidelong glance, smiling again, teasingly. "And maybe *this* time I'll find something even better."

I smack him over the head with my pillow.

We agree that I should have first choice of clothes, since

28

I'm going to school. As we get dressed, it occurs to me for the first time that we'll be using up my clean clothes twice as fast as usual. We're going to have to figure out some explanation for Mom, who'll notice it soon. But just as I'm about to mention it, the duplicate says, "I sure am hungry. That pizza wasn't very good last night."

"Me too," I say. And then the horrible realization hits me. Only one of us is going to be able to eat breakfast. I turn to the duplicate. "What are we going to do about eating?"

"I just thought of that," the duplicate says, looking blank. "I don't know."

We both sit down on the unmade beds, worried now. It wouldn't be so much of a problem if Mom had a regular job—then whoever didn't eat breakfast could snitch some food when everyone else had left the house. But Mom is an artist and works at home, making greeting cards with cute little kids on them, which are sold in the local shops. She has a studio next to the kitchen. She can certainly hear footsteps from in there, and cupboards being opened and closed.

And eating isn't the only problem. Whoever doesn't go to school won't even be able to stay at home; Mom would certainly find him. It doesn't matter so much now, while it's still reasonably warm out. But what about the winter when it will be really cold?

"Well," the duplicate finally says, after we've been brooding about the same things for several minutes. "I guess, whoever eats will just have to sneak some food and give it to the other one outside."

"Yeah, but putting bacon and eggs and buttered toast in our pockets isn't going to help the clothes situation,"

29

I point out. "Unless . . . I got an idea." I go to the closet and pull an old backpack off the shelf. "We'll just have to start carrying this every day, and steal food whenever we get the chance."

"I was just about to say the same thing myself," says the duplicate.

"Okay. But who gets to eat breakfast today?"

The duplicate thinks for a moment, and then smiles— that familiar phony smile that bothers me more every time I see it. "Whoever *doesn't* go to school should be the one to eat breakfast," the duplicate says. "Because whoever goes to school can be sure he'll get lunch; the one who doesn't go might not be able to."

I can't argue with that, as much as I'd like to. "All right, go down and eat then. I'll sneak out while you're all in the kitchen. Just be sure the news is loud enough so they won't hear me."

"Don't forget to make your bed," the duplicate says, still smiling, at the door.

"Why shouldn't you make yours too?"

"Because I was in the bed I always sleep in, which I never make, remember? It's the one *you* were in that has to look unused—so don't be sloppy about it." He takes the backpack from me. "I'll meet you out behind the garage; I'll do my best to get you a scrap or two."

I mutter angrily to myself as I make the bed. I try, but I can't come up with any unfairness in the way we're handling this situation. And yet somehow it seems that the duplicate always gets the better deal. Tonight I'll insist on switching beds so that the duplicate will have to do this chore tomorrow.

I sneak downstairs as quietly as possible, listening to the voices and TV from the kitchen. I have to use the front door, which is heavy and always rattles loudly when it's pulled shut. Outside on the porch, holding the knob in my hand, I try to decide whether to close and lock it. There is no way to do it quietly; you can always hear it all over the house. Finally, I pull it just as far as I can without making noise, so that it is only partially shut. I can't lock it, and will probably be blamed for that later. But I still don't dare to attract their attention.

I wait impatiently out behind the garage, standing in the building's shadow, ravenous now, looking at my watch every minute. I'm cold. The duplicate is wearing my leather jacket because Mom will see him leaving the house, and also he's going to be outside all day. I'm wearing a heavy sweater, but it's not enough. I look at my watch again. The duplicate is really taking his time in there. If he doesn't hurry I'll be late for school. I wonder how much food the duplicate will be able to sneak into the backpack.

"'Bye, see you later," I hear the duplicate say at last from the back door. A moment later he appears, wearing the backpack, carrying my books.

"What did you get?" I ask him immediately, reaching for the backpack.

"Now, just you wait a minute," the duplicate says pleasantly, fending me off. "Don't you want to know what we said at breakfast? Don't you want to know all the *details*?"

"Cut it out. You can tell me later. Just give me the food."

"I couldn't get very much; Mom kept watching me,"

the duplicate explains as he takes off the backpack, not sounding very apologetic. He hands me a banana and a piece of dry bread.

"That's *it*? Couldn't you do any better than that?"

"What did you expect me to do, put french toast and syrup in there?"

"She made french toast?" I mutter, gulping down the bread, which is stale and hard.

"And sausages—the good kind that I like so much," the duplicate helpfully informs me. "But I couldn't get any of them, either, or any orange juice or hot chocolate. Nothing to put them in. Come on, let's get away from the house before they see us." The duplicate starts off toward the street.

"You could have wrapped some sausages in paper towels or something," I complain, furiously peeling the banana as I hurry after him. "I would have thought of that."

"I did think of it. But Mom kept watching me, like I told you. Don't you want to know what we talked about?"

"Not particularly," I say, shoving the banana into my mouth and throwing the peel on the sidewalk. I don't usually litter, but I'm in such a lousy mood now that I hope somebody slips on it.

"Well, you have to know; it's kind of important."

"All right, what is it?" I say, through the banana, which is brown and mealy. Couldn't the duplicate have picked a better one?

"They thought I acted funny last night. You know, preoccupied at Grandma's, and afterwards changing my clothes and sneaking off for a walk, and then asking Dad that stupid question. They think I've got something on my mind that I don't have the nerve to talk about."

I sigh and roll my eyes. "So what did you tell them? You denied everything, right?"

"Wrong. I told them about Angela."

"Huh?" I stop and look hard at the duplicate. "Angela? What do you mean? What did you say about her?" I'm surprised, because it never would have occured to me to mention Angela to Mom and Dad today—and until now, the duplicate and I have always come up with the same solutions to things.

"I said she was pretty and I kind of liked her," the duplicate says smoothly, gesturing with one hand. "I said I was thinking about her at Grandma's. And I tried on those other clothes to see how good I looked in them. And I went for a walk because I wanted to be alone and think about her. And I asked Dad that question because Angela had asked me about clones, and I wanted to impress her."

We begin walking again. "I guess it doesn't sound *too* implausible," I say. "Did they fall for it?"

"Oh, sure. They thought it was real cute. And I just figured it would make more sense to give them an explanation than to deny everything. You know, to throw them off the track, so they won't get suspicious about *us*. Now whenever they think one of us is acting funny, we can use Angela as an excuse. She can also be the reason for going through clothes so fast. You know, wanting to look good for her. Brilliant, huh?"

I don't like him using Angela as an excuse. "I guess it was a smart thing to do," I have to admit, though I don't feel elated, as the duplicate obviously is. "Except, don't

33

you think it's peculiar that I never thought of telling them that? Usually we get the same ideas."

"You didn't think of telling them about Angela because you weren't with her last night, and I was. It makes sense that I'd be thinking about her more than you."

"Who says you think about her more than I do? Anyway, *I'll* be the one who sees her today."

"Yeah, I know," the duplicate says. "We'd better split up now." We stand and face each other on the sidewalk. "And try not to act funny, okay? I don't want Angela, or anybody else, to think there's anything peculiar about me."

"Don't worry about me; *I* know how to act," I say, insulted. "I just hope you told me everything that happened last night. If you left anything out, and I slip up—then it'll be your fault if she thinks I'm peculiar." I can't stand his attitude. "And I'm inviting her over after school. So you better not come home until five."

"She won't do it," he says instantly. "I mean . . . she might not want Carl to see her going off with you, in front of all the other kids."

"But you told me she said they're not going steady and she can do whatever she wants."

"I know." The duplicate looks uncomfortable now. "But last night, I also kind of got the idea she doesn't want to stop seeing Carl completely. At least until she knows me better."

"Why didn't you tell me that? Who does she like the best? You were supposed to tell me everything!"

He avoids the issue. "Anyway, you can't invite her over because you have band practice after school today, remember?"

He's right. "But I don't *want* to . . ." And then I have a brilliant idea. "Listen, you had all that time with her last night. So isn't it fair that I should have equal time with her too?"

"Well . . . I guess so," he says, chewing on his thumbnail, sounding suspicious.

"And we might as well take advantage of this crazy situation we're in. Otherwise, what good is it? So . . . I think you should go to band practice today."

"But you're the one who's going to be with Angela in school," he protests.

"It's not the same, just seeing her at school. And it's the perfect solution. Carl will be at band practice. He'll know you're there. He'll never be suspicious that I'm with her. It's exactly the kind of thing we should do for each other, being duplicates. It's like some crazy game. Come on." I like games, so he should too.

"Well, maybe," he says. "But what will people think, if they notice anything? And what'll you tell *her*?"

"I'll just tell her I know how to deal with Carl, that he'll remember seeing me at band practice because I'm always there. Post-hypnotic suggestion or something."

"Yeah, except . . . what if somebody notices I'm wearing different clothes?" He looks down at himself. "These clothes are sort of dumb-looking."

I'm surprised at how concerned he is with appearances. "Do you really think anybody will notice? Come on. Next time I'll do the same thing for you. I promise. If you don't help me this time, I won't help you out either."

He sighs. "Well, I hope nobody notices, but . . . all right, I'll go to band practice."

"Great, that's wonderful. I'll go out the front door, it's

35

closer to her locker. You come in the back. And I swear I'll do the same thing for you next time. You promise to be there?"

"Yeah, yeah, I won't let you down." He looks around nervously. "And now we *have* to split up, before somebody comes along. See you at five. And try not to make anybody suspicious, okay?"

"Sure. See you at five." We turn and walk away from each other.

I hope I'll be cool, but I don't feel as confident as I'd like. Of course I'm looking forward to seeing Angela. But I'm not sure what it's going to be like with her now, having to pretend I was with her last night. And as sure of myself as I tried to sound with the duplicate, I do feel a little guilty about playing such a trick on Carl—not to mention, will I really be able to convince Angela we can get away with it? It's going to be like putting on an act, all day long, and I hope I won't have any problems carrying it off.

6

I don't get a chance to talk to Angela before math class, which is third period. Carl's in this class too. None of us sits near each other. We hand in our problem sets, and for the next forty minutes I watch the teacher talking and writing things on the board, not hearing any of it. I keep wondering if I should walk Angela to our fourth period class, or stay away from her because of Carl. It doesn't help that the duplicate was so vague and so reluctant to tell me what Angela said about Carl last night. I don't want to hurt her feelings by ignoring her, but I also don't want to make Carl suspicious. I'm angry at the duplicate for putting me in this situation. Why can't he understand how important it is to tell each other everything?

Bored as I am, the bell rings sooner than I expect, probably because I can't decide what to do. Ordinarily I would just say hi to her without even thinking about it, but now I feel awkward, not cool at all. It's the duplicate's fault. I take a long time getting my books and papers together, so that I'm one of the last people out of the room.

Angela and Carl are standing in the corridor, near the wall, out of the way of the hurtling masses. Angela turns and smiles at me. She looks even prettier than I remember, a blue sweater intensifying the color of her eyes. "Hi, David," she says. "Did you finish all those stupid problems?"

She knows I finished the problems, since the duplicate essentially did them for her. The only reason she's asking me is to make it clear that Carl isn't supposed to know we were together last night. But she doesn't seem nervous about it; she actually seems to be enjoying our complicity. "I had trouble with a couple," I say.

"You? The great math brain?" Carl asks, lifting his eyebrows. His tone seems to imply that being good at math is a trivial accomplishment.

"I like your sweater, David," Angela says quickly.

"Looks like polyester," says Carl. "I thought you only liked clothes made out of natural fibers, Angela."

"On myself, I do," she admits. "Come on, David, we'll be late for history."

"See you at lunch," says Carl, who's in a different class this period. He puts his hand briefly on her shoulder. I have to admit that they make a striking couple, Angela being a redhead, Carl very tall with curly black hair and dark eyes. And his shirt looks like it's 100 percent pure wool. I remind myself that I'm not bad-looking either, judging from the duplicate's appearance this morning.

"I really had a great time last night," I tell Angela as we start down the hall.

"Yeah. Too bad Damon was such a pest, interrupting us all the time." She rolls her eyes. "He's worse than my

38

parents. It would have been better if *he* was the one who went out and they'd been at home."

"Really?" I say stupidly. It's the first I've heard about her parents not being home last night. And what were she and the duplicate doing that her older brother Damon, who's a senior, kept interrupting? I silently curse the duplicate. How much more did he leave out?

"Yeah. He *always* treats me like I'm five years old. By the way, what were you two talking about while I was on the phone with Carl? You must have been pretty involved to let the pizza almost burn."

"Oh. Ummm . . . just school and things," I say, wanting to punch the duplicate. How could he do this to me?

"Yeah, but what were you laughing so hard about? Sounded like you were having a great time."

"Oh, ahhh, your brother just kept telling jokes," I improvise, feeling like I'm walking a tightrope in the dark. "You have to admit, he has a good sense of humor."

"Telling jokes?" she says, giving me a funny look. "I've never heard Damon tell a joke in my life."

"Well, you know, they were like, um, *male* jokes. I mean, I guess he probably doesn't talk that way in front of you."

"Like what? Give me an example."

"Oh, um, I . . . can't seem to remember any. I can never remember jokes."

"*Male* jokes, huh?" She's looking straight ahead now, not smiling. "I'll have to get him to tell me some."

"He probably won't. Listen, Angela, are you doing

anything after school today?" I say quickly to change the subject.

"No, I'm not—like I told you when you asked me last night." She's actually frowning at me now. "Are you coming down with Alzheimer's or something? You don't seem to be able to remember *anything* today."

"Well, would you like to come over to my house?" I ask her, avoiding the memory issue. "I don't have any brothers or sisters to pester us."

She brightens for a moment. "Sure, David, I'd like to see . . ." Then she sighs. "Except Carl will probably want to walk me home. His locker's right across the hall from mine."

"No, he won't. He has band practice after school today."

"Yeah, but then *you* have band practice too."

"That's the whole beauty of it," I say, trying to sound convincing. But what I'm really feeling is desperate, because suddenly I can't find any logic to hold onto. "I mean, Carl will expect me to be there. And if he thinks I'm there, then how can he think I'm with you? Get it?"

Angela laughs, less out of amusement than at the absurdity of what I'm saying. "You really have a peculiar mind, David, you know that? If he's expecting you to be there, then he'll notice that you're *not* there. He'll wonder what happened to you. He'll ask about it." She shakes her head, puzzled.

We stop outside the door of our next class. "Believe me, Angela, he'll think I was in band. The power of suggestion, and all that. It's happened with him before. He gets different days mixed up or something. That's the way he is."

40

"You sound like you know him better than I do."

"Look, just meet me after school, across the street from the statue," I say as the bell rings.

I worry during the rest of my classes. What if she doesn't meet me? I wouldn't blame her if she stood me up. The whole idea about Carl believing I'm in band must sound totally preposterous to her. Why did I ever think it would make sense? Maybe the situation is making me a little irrational. And what if the duplicate doesn't go to band? I have no reason to believe that he will, or to trust him at all, now that I know how much he left out about what he and Angela did last night. He couldn't have made it any worse if he'd purposely set me up to blunder with her—and maybe that *was* his plan. But it's senseless, because if she thinks I'm a jerk, she'll think he's a jerk too.

Worst of all, I keep wondering about what happened between the two of them at her house, with her parents not there. For some reason, I'm a lot more jealous of the duplicate than I am of Carl. The thought of any intimacy between Angela and the duplicate bothers me horribly. Still, painful as it is, I can't stop thinking about it. I've got to find out everything, even if it hurts. But how can I? I can't ask Angela. And I don't know how to get the duplicate to tell me.

After school, I wait across the street from the statue of George Washington that's in front of the main entrance, forcing myself not to watch the front doors of the building constantly to see if she's coming. I picture the duplicate sneaking into band through the back door, hoping that if I imagine it hard enough it might really be happening. Then I begin to worry that he and Angela might run into each other inside; that possibility did not occur to me until now.

I see her coming down the steps in her green parka. I turn away, trying not to appear too eager or impatient. In a minute I turn back to see her approaching me. I do my best to smile calmly.

She grins back at me, apparently in a good mood again. "I hope you and Carl are having a good time in band," she says.

"Oh, we are," I assure her, falling in step beside her. "Carl's watching me during the rests so he knows when to come in, instead of counting the measures himself, just like he always does."

"Typical." She shakes her head and giggles. "I can't wait to ask him about it. I've got to tell you, David, I'll really be surprised if he thinks you were there."

"We'll see," I say, hoping I look smug.

"Yeah, we'll see," she says, her smile fading a little. "But if I really cared what he thought, I wouldn't be going with you."

"Really?" I say. I want to encourage her to talk about him, since I'm curious about her feelings. But I can't ask her anything specific because I don't know what she told the duplicate about him last night.

"In a way, I'd almost be glad if he found out I'm going over to your house. I told you what a jerk he can be about me and other boys."

"Yeah, I remember," I lie. "The real jealous type."

"It really bothers me," she says. "He gets so mad when I want to be at all friendly with anybody else. It's like he's forcing me to lie to him and sneak around behind his back. And I don't like being that way; I don't like him

42

controlling me. I'd much rather be honest about it. In fact, from now on I'm going to be." She sticks her lower lip out slightly, which makes her look like a little girl.

I feel encouraged by what she's saying. "I guess what really matters is how *you* feel about it," I tell her. "Do you want him to know you're doing things with me, or not?"

"I don't want him to make me feel like a criminal about it," she says, staring ahead and still pouting. "I don't know, David; I'm just not sure how I feel," she says, looking up at me again, her eyes wide. "I mean, I do like a lot of things about him. I don't want to lie to you. But I get tired of just being with *him* all the time. And I can't stand the way he's so jealous. Are *you* jealous?"

"Well, I'm not jealous of Carl," I tell her honestly.

"Good," she says, beginning to smile again.

Her eyes are huge; she has a dimple beside each corner of her mouth. I feel such a rush of affection for her that I'd do anything just for the chance to be with her. But I can't put the feeling into words; it would sound sappy.

We reach my house. Of course Mom is at home. Angela turns out to be absolutely fascinated by Mom's studio and the cards she's working on. It seems that Angela would like to be an artist herself. They do most of the talking for a while, and I stand there feeling extremely proud and happy, trying not to stare at Angela too much. But Angela smiles whenever she finds my eyes on her. We have a snack in the kitchen, and I think of all sorts of questions to ask Angela about her drawing and painting. I completely forget about the duplicate; I feel nothing but the warm glow of being with Angela.

Until I happen to notice that it's a quarter to five. The

43

duplicate will be back soon. Instantly everything changes. I'm a nervous wreck. I don't know what to do. Angela's probably expecting me to drive her home in Mom's car, but what if the duplicate shows up while I'm gone? We made no arrangements about how he would get into the house; neither of us thought about it.

"What's the matter, David? You look funny."

"I just remembered something," I tell her. "I've got an errand to do before five. I'd better drive you home."

"What's the rush?" Angela says. "Is it really that important?"

"I'll tell you all about it, uh, tomorrow," I say, standing up. "I've got to get the keys."

Angela keeps looking at me in the car. But she doesn't seem critical or suspicious, just curious and a little amused. I seem to have made a good impression on her. "You sure are a mysterious person, David," she says, as she gets out. "I never expected you to be so full of surprises."

"Oh, uh, thanks," I say. "See you tomorrow."

"I can't wait to see what Carl has to say," she says, grinning, as she slams the door.

The traffic is terrible on the way back. At five o'clock I'm sitting in a long line of cars at a red light, bouncing up and down on the seat, groaning aloud. I don't get home until a quarter past, frantic and sweating. I rush inside, slamming the front door behind me.

"Who's that?" I hear Mom say, from the kitchen.

"Oh, uh, I guess I didn't completely close the door," the duplicate loudly tells her. "It must have been the wind." He peeks out into the hallway and brusquely motions at me to get upstairs.

"I still don't understand how you got back home so

44

fast," Mom says, as soon as he goes back into the kitchen. "You must have been driving like a maniac. If you don't drive more carefully, we'll have to take away your car privileges, you know. And why do you keep leaving the door open?" She continues to lecture him as I creep upstairs. She must be so upset that she hasn't yet noticed he's wearing different clothes.

It's another close call, as bad as last night, and I can't stand the strain and tension of it. And yet I see now, with a hopeless despair I've never felt before, that situations like this are going to keep happening every day, as long as the duplicate is around. There is no way we can avoid them. I'll be living with constant stress and anxiety from now on. But I can't take it; I'll never get used to it. It's already starting to make me feel a little crazy. I wish I had never made the duplicate. It just isn't worth it.

The duplicate enters the room, grinning at me as though nothing is the matter. "Listen, you won't believe what I found," he begins eagerly. "It's the answer to—"

"Why weren't you more careful?" I whisper. "You should have checked first. We almost got caught again. And what about last night? What are you trying to put over on me? And did you go to band? Did Carl see you?"

The duplicate's smile fades only a little. He holds up his hand, patting the air in a comforting gesture. "Calm down, calm down, everything's going to be okay now," he says.

The duplicate's manner only makes me more angry. "No, it isn't okay. Everything's impossible. And it's all your fault. I *demand* to know why you lied to me about what happened at Angela's last night."

"Lied?" the duplicate says, looking hurt. "I might be

45

a little forgetful sometimes, but I'm not a liar. You know that."

"*I'm* not a liar—I know that. So why can't you be honest with me?"

"I *am* honest with you," the duplicate says, shrugging, as though it's a trivial issue. Then he brightens. "Don't you want to hear what I found? It's the solution to all our problems—it really is."

Why can't the duplicate understand what I'm trying to say? Is it possible that he's *not* intentionally dishonest, that he's just out of touch with reality? The idea that he might be slightly crazy is almost more disturbing than his deliberately hiding things from me. "There's no solution. Everything's a mess," I say bitterly.

"No, it isn't. Everything's fine now." The duplicate pushes himself away from the desk and approaches me, beaming again. "A hideout, a secret hideout for us. And I'm taking you there right now."

Luckily, Mom goes out to do an errand. The duplicate crams a sleeping bag and flashlight, crackers and peanut butter and cookies into the backpack and leaves the house first. I wait for a few minutes, then hurry to the beach to meet the duplicate there—obviously it isn't safe to walk together on the street. The duplicate has been secretive about exactly what this hideout is, telling me he wants it to be a surprise. I know the beach as well as the duplicate, and can't imagine what place he might be thinking of— the beach is a protected wildlife area; no one can build houses or even camp out overnight there. And I trust the duplicate less than ever now. This is probably just some nasty trick; I warn myself to be prepared for anything.

When I reach him, the duplicate is poking through the richly organic beach debris with a stick, just the way I always do. "Come on. I can't wait to show it to you," he says, pushing the stick into a jellyfish (which I *wouldn't* do) and dropping it. We start off quickly across the damp sand.

"How far away is this place?" I ask him.

"Not far."

"But what is it? It's some place I know about, isn't it? It's got to be."

"You'll see."

"Well, I just hope you're not making this all up," I say.

"I'm telling you, it's perfect. Wait'll you see. I know you'll be as excited as I am."

I hope so. A workable hideout would be a solution to a lot of our problems; I saw that right away. It would be a place for one of us to stay while the other is at school. We could keep food there. Maybe we could even take turns sleeping there, instead of both sneaking around in the house at the same time, constantly afraid of being discovered. But I try not to let my hopes get too high.

We head away from the water, into the dunes, and up a steep rocky slope. Then I see the forbidding concrete structure rising up at the top of the hill, and stop hoping. I freeze, grabbing the duplicate's arm. "*That* place?" I say, my voice a thin squeak against the wet rumble of surf. "If this is some kind of a joke, it's not funny."

"No joke. Come on." The duplicate pulls free of me and clambers up onto a boulder. He turns back, the wind lifting his hair, his face dark in the building's shadow. "Come on! You don't know what it's like. You've never even been inside."

"You went *in* there?" I ask him, frightened, but also a little curious.

"Yeah, I went in there. And it's better than you ever thought. Wait'll you see."

"I don't *want* to see," I say. But I start after him again.

48

It is the old army watchtower from World War II, where men were stationed to keep a lookout for enemy ships and planes. A four-story-high square structure, bleak and unadorned, it has only a few narrow openings for windows. Apparently that was to prevent any lights inside from showing, so that the building would be invisible from sea or air. It also means, I realize, that any lights inside could easily be hidden if I were staying there at night.

Not that I can imagine staying there alone at night; the idea is too terrifying to contemplate. Despite the fact that it's an empty, abandoned building, just asking to be used as a hangout away from the prying eyes of parents, no teenagers in town ever have parties in it anymore, even the wilder ones. A boy was murdered here once, in some horrible way that made the police think it must have been done by a psychotic. They never found out who did it— the place is so isolated they didn't even discover the body for days. I don't know much about the case; I was only a little kid at the time. I just know that no one ever considers breaking into the tower now.

No one, that is, but the duplicate, who is just disappearing around the edge of the building. I run after him, cursing him, the wind cold on the back of my neck. I find him beside a piece of plywood leaning against the wall that faces away from the sea. He's dragging the plywood along the wall. "Well, don't just stand there," he calls over his shoulder. "Come on, help me out. This thing weighs a ton."

I hurry over and struggle with the plywood, feeling conspicuous. We move it to the side, then prop it against the wall. The duplicate studies it for a moment. "Might be better if it looks like the wind blew it over," he says, and suddenly pushes it away from the building. I just manage to get out of the way, and when it hits the ground, the impact sends dust and grit into my eyes.

The plywood was covering a tarnished metal door with a padlock. "Lock was so old and rusty, all I had to do was bang it with a stone and it fell apart," the duplicate says, lifting the lock out of the door. "We'll get a new one tomorrow, to keep anybody else out—so we won't have to worry about what happened here before." He turns his back to me. "Get the flashlight out of the pack. The sun'll be down in a minute."

I obey. "But I'm still not sure I want . . . to do this," I mumble.

"Look, we don't have any choice. If we don't have a hideout, we'll be in trouble, fast. You know that. Can you come up with any other place?"

"Maybe," I say, though I doubt it. I know the duplicate is right: We have to have a hideout. If only it could be someplace else!

"Give me that." The duplicate takes the flashlight and pushes at the door. It squeals, and the sea gulls circling above us answer back. As it opens, a pathway of orange light from the sun, setting behind us, stretches out across the dark cement floor, on which I can see the duplicate's earlier sandy footprints, and pebbles and paper cups and dead leaves that have blown inside, and our two identical elongated shadows.

"Come on," the duplicate says, and steps into the building. I follow him.

The duplicate turns to shut the door, and anticipating my protest says, "Just in case anybody comes along, so they won't know we're inside."

The sunlight shrinks and vanishes. I can see nothing until the duplicate, after waiting a long moment, switches on the flashlight.

"Well, here we are," the duplicate announces, in an unnaturally loud voice.

"You think this is perfect?" I say, my eyes following the pale circle of light around the barren and filthy room. There are old newspapers on the floor, an overturned table, and several dented metal chairs. A large black contraption squats in one corner, sprouting pipes, flanked by some other pieces of equipment that look electrical, all of it old-fashioned, coated thickly with dust and draped with cobwebs.

"Come on. This way," the duplicate says, moving off to the right. I follow him through a doorway to a metal stairway. We climb side by side; the stairway turns, and we reach the second floor. The duplicate passes the doorway that opens off the landing on the second floor and starts up the next flight.

I stop beside the door. "What's in here?" I ask him.

"I don't know, I haven't checked it out yet," the duplicate says, continuing up the stairs. I follow. On the third floor he leads me off the landing, down a narrow corridor, and through the second doorway on the right. He stops just inside and moves the flashlight around the small room.

There are two narrow metal beds in here, against the walls on the left and right, and one of them even has a mattress on it, thin and stained and torn in places, grayish stuffing leaking out. Between the beds a small sink protrudes from the wall, the pipes exposed, the enamel cracked and blackened. A metal table stands between the sink and the bed on the left, which is the one with the mattress. The duplicate sets the flashlight on the table, so that the beam illuminates the bed. He shrugs off the backpack, takes the food out and puts it on the table, and tosses the sleeping bag onto the bed. He turns and smiles at me. "What did I tell you? All the comforts of home. The bathroom's down at the end of the hall."

I don't know what to say. Yes, there's a bed and four walls. And it doesn't really matter so much that the place is cold and filthy, as cheerless as a prison cell. What bothers me is that the building is so isolated, and so dark, and has so many rooms and floors, and no security at all. I can't forget what happened here. A person alone would be totally vulnerable. I absolutely cannot conceive of staying here overnight by myself; I refuse.

Still, the duplicate can be very persuasive, and very stubborn. What if he announces that one of us has to stay here tonight, and we have to flip a coin? What would I do then? I don't know what I would do.

And what is almost as frightening as the idea of staying here alone is the fact that the duplicate doesn't seem to be afraid of the place. How is that possible if he really is an exact copy of me?

But he isn't. With a terrible feeling of foreboding, I admit to myself that he has been a little different from me all along. He's more stubborn; he's done several things I never would have done, such as coming to this tower.

52

And since he *isn't* a totally accurate copy of me, there will probably be other differences too—unexpected differences—that I won't be prepared for.

Then I notice the Spee-Dee-Dupe under the bed. "How'd you get that thing here already?" I ask him.

"I snuck back and got it first thing as soon as I found this place."

It's not the first thing I would have done. "Don't you think that was pretty risky? What if Mom caught you?"

"Well, she didn't. And I know it was risky, but it was important enough to be worth it. I had to get it out of the house as soon as I found a safe place for it. What if Mom found it and accidentally made a copy of herself? Can you imagine that, two Moms?" He smiles, trying to make a joke of it. "Well, what do you think of our hideout?"

"I don't like it. I could never stay here."

"Oh, come on," the duplicate says. "We can fix it up. It'll be fun. Tomorrow when I'm in school, you should really finish checking out the place; see what's on the second floor. And start cleaning it up a little. I'll come and help as soon as I get out of school. And we can get some camping equipment, like an oil lamp and maybe one of those little stoves, so we can make hot chocolate. And a radio and tape player, and cards and books and games. A real hideout. Think about it. We can do *anything we want* here, and no one will know about it."

"And if we get murdered, no one will know about it either," I say. "If you really are the same as me, with all the same memories and feelings, then you have to understand why I don't want to stay here. You can't have

53

turned into a completely different person after only one day on your own—unless you never *were* the same as me."

The duplicate watches me for a moment. "Well, yes, it *is* scary," he finally admits. "And I only had the nerve to come here by myself because it was the middle of the afternoon. I never could have come here without you at this time of day. Sure, I know how you feel. I feel it too."

Is the duplicate really being sincere, or is he just feeding me a line to make me *think* we're the same? I have no way of knowing. I can only hope he's telling the truth, for the moment. "Well, okay," I say. "So if that's the way you feel, then what's all this stuff about fixing it up, since you know neither of us wants to stay here alone? Were you hoping *I* would stay here by myself, and you wouldn't have to?"

"No, I wasn't," the duplicate says. He looks behind him, and then sits down rather gingerly on the bed. "It's just that we have to have a hideout; we're going to get caught if we keep staying at home together. And I can't think of anyplace else. I was hoping if we fixed this place up, and spent enough time here together to get used to it, then we'd both get comfortable enough to take turns sleeping here. Doesn't that make sense?"

"So you weren't thinking one of us would have to stay here tonight?" I can't prevent myself from asking, relief showing in my voice.

The duplicate smiles slowly. "So *that's* what's making you so nervous." He shakes his head and clucks his teeth. "I should have known. I guess that's what I would have been afraid of, too, if you'd been the one to find this place. Except . . ." He pauses and stares hard at me. "You know what that means? It means you really were afraid I could somehow make you stay here, even though you didn't want to." He stands up, speaking quietly, his face lit from below by the flashlight on the table in the dark room. "And *that* means I'm the one in control."

"No!" I shout. I step forward and grab the flashlight from the table. "I'm getting out of here." I turn and walk out of the room.

"Running away won't change anything," the duplicate says, following me.

"I'm not running away. I just wanted to see how fast you'd come after me if I took the light. You can't make me do anything. You're just putting on an act, pretending to be so tough and brave and in control. You don't like the dark either. It's the one with the light who's in control, that's all." I start down the metal stairs, slippery with sand and stones.

"All right, so you have the light. But who eats supper tonight? Why don't we have a polite little discussion on that topic?"

"I eat supper, of course. You're starting to forget things. You're the one who ate breakfast. So I get supper."

"But you had lunch!" the duplicate argues, pounding

56

down the stairs behind me. "I haven't had anything since this morning. We agreed to take turns."

"We are taking turns." I reach the bottom of the stairs, kick a mildewed roll of toilet paper out of the way, and head for the door. I have to get home before the duplicate does, and be seen by Mom and Dad first, or else I won't be able to eat. "You were the last one to eat a meal at home," I say. "Now it's my turn. Anyway, you were free to do anything you wanted all day long. You could have gotten a sandwich somewhere. And I'll be sure to get a lot of food for your supper—just the way you got me that huge delicious breakfast this morning."

"I got you as much as I could. And anyway, I'm going to school tomorrow, so that means you'll get to eat breakfast in the morning; so that means I should get to eat supper tonight."

I push open the door and step out. It's so dark in the building that I expect it to be dark outside, but there's still a little light. The duplicate puts the ruined lock back in place, and we both pick up the plywood and position it over the door. While I'm still struggling with it, the duplicate lets go suddenly and backs away. "You get to eat supper, huh? We'll see about that. If I get there first, what'll you be able to do about it? Nothing!" He laughs and takes off down the slope.

A gust of wind almost tears the plywood out of my hands, and I wrestle with it, grunting, until I manage to get it back up against the wall in a somewhat secure position. By then, the duplicate has reached the bottom of the slope and is already tearing away across the beach.

"Stop! You can't do this!" I yell after him uselessly, as I stumble and slide down the steep incline.

It's difficult to run on the soft sand, and I'm out of breath after twenty yards. My only consolation is that the duplicate has to be out of breath too, since he's in the same physical shape as I am. The sun has fallen behind the dunes now; the duplicate is a vague dark figure on the twilit beach, but he does seem to be slowing down. I put out an extra burst of speed to try to catch up with him. The duplicate slows to a walk. I'm closing in on him. Then the duplicate turns, sees me approaching, and begins running again. By the time I reach the street, the duplicate has rounded the corner, two blocks ahead, and is out of sight. I'll never catch up with him. I stop running.

It's a dirty trick the duplicate has pulled, a really nasty thing to do. Up until now we've made all decisions fairly, discussing them, taking turns, flipping coins. But now the duplicate has changed all that. Will we ever go back to being rational and civilized after this? Or is it going to be a hostile, warlike free-for-all from now on?

"Well, if it is, it'll be his fault," I mutter. I say it aloud because I know it's not true. Back in the tower, I also decided to try to beat the duplicate back to the house. I just didn't move fast enough, that's the only difference. Next time I'll have to be more on my toes.

It's six forty-five when I reach the house, and we always eat exactly at seven o'clock, when the news is over. Dad is in the living room, Mom in the kitchen, and I can't safely enter the house until they're all at the table. I have to wait outside behind the garage again, cold and hungry again, ineffectually cursing the duplicate.

I'm tired of getting the raw deal every time. I won't tolerate it any more; I have to take some action to change the pattern. And by the time I go inside, I know what to do. The duplicate, at least, did not close the front door completely, so I can get in without attracting attention. Not that the duplicate did it to be nice to me; it's for his own protection too. I go quietly across the front hall to the stairs.

"You're really tucking into that steak," Dad is saying in the kitchen, amid the rattle of silverware and the smells of broiled meat and melted cheese. "Better slow down or you'll get indigestion."

"It's just so delicious," the duplicate says thickly, his mouth full. I hear him swallow and gulp down milk. "And these potatoes are *great!*"

"I put cheese in the scalloped potatoes, real Gruyère," Mom says. "I'm glad you like them."

I creep up the stairs, salivating, consumed by rage at the duplicate. I know I shouldn't make this phone call, that it's a risky and foolhardy thing to do and will probably get me into a lot of trouble. But I don't care now; I'm determined to get back at the duplicate at any cost. And this is what *I* want to do. I go into my room and close the door. Without even pausing to think about it, I pick up the phone and dial Angela's number.

I'm in luck; Angela answers. "Hi, how're you doing, it's me, David," I say.

"Oh . . . hi," she says. "David, how did you *do* that?"

"Do what?" I'm so furious at the duplicate, I have no idea what she's talking about.

"How did you make Carl think you were in band today? He called up, and I didn't want to just ask him, so I told

59

him I thought I saw you right after school on a new BMW cycle. He said it had to be somebody else, that you were next to him in band. David, you're amazing! What did you do, hypnotize him or something?"

My mood changes slightly. At least the duplicate did something I asked him to, for a change. Finally we pulled a trick on somebody that worked.

"Well, how did you do it? He said you never stopped talking about me."

Now I'm angry at him again. Why did he have to talk to Carl about Angela? "I'll tell you tomorrow. Listen, I just had the craziest idea," I say, concentrating on how furious and disappointed the duplicate will be if this thing works. "Skip school tomorrow and meet me at the beach."

There is silence on the other end. Finally she says, "You're right, it is a crazy idea."

"I'm telling you, there's no thrill like doing something crazy," I plunge ahead. "It's a great feeling to think of everybody else stuck in school while we're running around having fun. We can make sand castles, have a picnic, fly kites. We could go to the movies and eat popcorn and candy too. We'll forge notes, the whole bit. I'm good at it. So what about it?"

Again, Angela doesn't respond for a moment. I hold my breath. Then she giggles. "I never had you pegged as the wild type, David. I'm *shocked*. . . . Where do we meet? What time?"

"At ten, by that old watchtower on the beach."

"The watchtower?" She doesn't like that idea.

"Sure. Nobody will see us there. It's perfect."

"Well . . . all right," she reluctantly agrees.

"And remember, we're both dead if anyone finds out about this."

"No problem. I know how to keep my mouth shut. I'll just play sick until Mom and Dad go to work. It'll be easy, as long as I get home before Damon does."

"Great, Angela. See you then."

Now my anger is gone completely. I feel elated and very excited. Angela must really like me a lot! She is going to risk getting in trouble to spend the day with me. And she actually seemed to be impressed that I suggested doing something that was against the rules. As little as I know her, I've managed to come up with exactly the kind of thing that will intrigue her.

And, of course, there is the added gleeful pleasure of knowing that for the second day in a row, I—not the duplicate—will be with Angela. So what if the duplicate gets to eat tonight? I'm getting Angela, and she's a lot more important than one meal. I can just imagine the expression on the duplicate's face when he gets to school tomorrow and finds out Angela isn't there. He'll know immediately that she's with me, and he won't be able to do a thing about it. It wasn't a mistake to call her; it was exactly the right thing to do.

But I have to pretend I'm still angry when the duplicate comes up to the room—if he notices how happy I am, he'll know something is up. And so when the duplicate, looking a little worried, steps through the door with the backpack in his hand, I say, "Come on, give me the food. And you better have plenty. It took you long enough."

"Sure. It's right here." The duplicate begins to unzip the backpack. Then he glances away, avoiding looking directly at me, his manner hesitant. "I guess . . . maybe it wasn't fair what I did," he says and sighs. "I'm sorry. I know we should have worked it out more reasonably."

"Forget the phony apology and give me the food," I demand, almost enjoying myself. Apparently the duplicate doesn't realize I wanted to beat him to supper too, and so now he feels guilty. As a result, I can be morally superior. It's immensely satisfying.

"I offered to do the dishes; that's why it took me so long to get up here." He finishes unzipping the backpack. "I figured if I was alone in the kitchen, I could get more food for you. I hope it's enough." He carefully takes out two plastic bags and sets them on the desk.

Now I feel a little less superior. Washing the dishes was a definite sacrifice; I'm not sure I would have done it. But I keep up my act, rudely not answering or looking at the duplicate as I march over to the desk. One bag contains a paper plate with a hefty chunk of steak on it and a pile of potatoes. In the other bag is a large piece of chocolate cake. The duplicate has even thought to include a plastic knife and fork and a napkin.

I pick up the steak and gnaw into it. Now I'm beginning to feel guilty myself. Maybe what the duplicate did really wasn't so unfair. After all, only one of us can eat with my parents, and I *did* devour a big lunch at school, and the duplicate hasn't eaten anything since breakfast. Now he's gone to a lot of trouble to get this food for me. He really does seem to feel genuinely contrite; his actions prove it.

And what have I done? I sneakily called up Angela and made this unnecessary arrangement with her which could very well lead to exposure for both of us. This is a lot more dangerous than just having the duplicate go to band after school while I'm with Angela. Tomorrow he'll be in all of our classes, all day long. *Everybody* we both know will see him. Angela will have to have an explanation—I won't be able to tell her I gave a post-hypnotic suggestion to everybody we know.

And the duplicate didn't do anything treacherous and selfish like that on his day off from school. He found a hideout for us. The more I think about it (as I eat the chocolate cake), the more it begins to seem that I'm the villain and the duplicate the innocent victim.

Before we go to bed, I tell the duplicate a lot about what happened with Angela during the day. It makes me feel even guiltier, because I'm leaving out the most important fact of all, that I'm skipping school with Angela tomorrow behind the duplicate's back. I feel so guilty, and so worried about the possible consequences of being with Angela while the duplicate is in school all day, that I sleep very little and wake up just as it's getting light.

I'm too restless to stay in bed for another minute. If I get up and do something constructive, maybe I won't feel so bad. I can get a broom and some other stuff, and go over to the tower and begin cleaning up the little bedroom there, as the duplicate suggested. And maybe later, I can get my hands on some money and pick up a camping light too. That might make up, at least partially, for the low trick I'm pulling today.

As I'm getting a piece of paper to write a note, I glance at the aquarium. One of the fish is swimming around, opening and closing its mouth as usual. The other one

63

keeps banging into the glass wall, as if he's trying to swim through it. I've never seen a fish behave like that. Are fish smart enough to go crazy? I study him, and I notice he looks different from the other one now. There's a black mark behind his gills, like a line drawn with a felt-tipped pen, and another mark on one of his fins that wasn't there before. I wonder briefly which fish is the original and which is the duplicate.

My duplicate is sleeping peacefully. I leave him a note which says, "I'm going to the tower to start cleaning. Won't be here for breakfast. Have a good day at school." I get out of the house without incident, carrying a broom and a bucket with cleaning fluids and old towels and rags in it, and a shopping bag packed with a pair of jeans and a T-shirt so I won't get my good clothes dirty—I would have brought my really old sweat pants and sweat shirt, but Mom must have thrown them away, as she's been threatening to do for months.

It's beautiful at the beach in the early morning, the sun rising over the water, and I begin to feel a little more cheerful. Maybe seeing Angela today won't mess things up; maybe I can get away with it—and if I do, I won't try anything this stupid again.

Even the tower doesn't seem so terrifying at this time of day. I push the plywood to the ground and open the door. It's not very bright inside, but I can see without the flashlight. If anything, the building seems even crummier by daylight, all the grit and grime and litter clearer and more sharp-edged than in the evening. But the place will look a lot better when I get through with it.

I start up the stairs, carrying the cleaning equipment in

both hands. On the second floor, I notice that the wooden door that leads from the landing is slightly ajar. I haven't seen what's through this door, and the duplicate said he hadn't been in there either. He urged me to check it out. I put down the broom and the bucket. Standing on the threshold, I push the door open.

And release a large heavy object that has been carefully balanced on the top of the door.

I watch for Angela from the fourth floor observation
room. I hurry downstairs and outside as soon as she appears at the end of the beach, so she won't know I was
inside the tower. I walk slowly toward her, poking around
with a stick, hoping she won't notice how frightened I
still am about what happened at the tower four hours ago.

"Hi!" I call out when she's close enough to hear, smiling and waving at her with the stick.

"What's the stick for? Were you looking for something?" she calls back.

"I was just poking around, that's all," I explain as she
approaches. "I always think I might find a bottle with a
message in it."

She stops beside me and looks at me as if I'm nuts, but
she is also smiling. "I never know what you're going to
say next, David, that's for sure." She turns and looks out
at the ocean. "Well, here we are at the beach. Now what
do we do?"

Suddenly I wish I'd done more thinking before calling her up last night. It sounded like such a wild exploit then. But now I'm responsible for coming up with exciting things for us to do together all day, to make sure we'll have a great time. At least I'm not stupid enough to consider taking her inside the tower and showing her how I'm fixing it up, as much as I'd like to. Whatever is going to happen between me and the duplicate now, it will only complicate matters if Angela knows about our secret hideout.

"We'll go exploring up the beach, we'll go farther than we've ever been before; maybe we really will find a message in a bottle," I say, trying to sound enthusiastic. "We'll get some sun and work up an appetite. Then we'll get something to eat. Then we'll go to the movies and eat all the disgusting junk food we want. Unless there's something else you want to do."

"No . . . that sounds okay," she says. I've been worried she might be disappointed that we're not doing anything really wild, but she seems reasonably satisfied. "I like to walk. And I've never been past the tower; nobody else I was with ever wanted to get *this* close to it." She turns and looks at it for the first time now, then quickly back to me.

"So what are we waiting for?" I say, and we start off. It's easy to talk to her. Breaking the rules together makes us both feel freer about discussing certain things, such as problems with parents.

Angela has a lot to say about her parents being too restrictive—even though, from what I can tell, they seem a lot *less* restrictive than many parents. She tells me how suspicious her brother Damon was this morning when she said she was sick, and criticizes him again for being overprotective of her. I listen and make comments, and joke and smile.

She asks me how I pulled the trick on Carl yesterday; I tell her it was a post-hypnotic suggestion—I learned how to do it from a comic book. She tells me that Carl is not as good a listener as I am, that she's beginning to realize how limited and dull he is. She thinks she might not want to go out with him at all anymore.

When Angela stumbles behind some boulders, I grab her shoulders, and she holds her face close to mine and I kiss her, wondering if the duplicate kissed her the other night. She kisses back and doesn't pull away. It's the longest kiss of my life. "You're beautiful," I whisper into her ear.

And the whole time I'm thinking about what happened four hours ago.

There's an ugly scraping sound above me as I open the door. I jump backwards. A large concrete block misses my head by inches and slams into the floor.

I stare down at it, the sharp crack of its impact ringing in my ears. Then the reaction hits—my heart speeding, the sick feeling in my stomach, the burst of sweat. I back up, knocking over the bucket, and sink down on a step. The block has chipped the cement floor. It would easily have crushed my head if it had hit me.

It almost killed me! And I escaped—this time. But it might happen again. And it might keep on happening as long as the duplicate exists.

Is it possible that it *wasn't* the duplicate who put the

concrete block there? Maybe some homicidal prankster—like the one who killed that teenager—set it up weeks or months ago. The duplicate told me he had never been through this door. Maybe it's the truth. In a way, it's hard to believe that the duplicate would actually try to kill me, as obnoxious as he is at times. It's so crazily extreme, so unreal; ordinary people don't go around trying to smash other people's heads in.

But the duplicate isn't an ordinary person. He's a machine-made copy of a person. He might be trying to kill me. I've got to be realistic about it. And if he *did* put the block there, then what else is he going to do?

I start to panic. Are there other booby traps? The whole place might be full of them; the duplicate was here all day yesterday. I'm vulnerable on the open stairway, with all that empty space and two more landings above me. I lurch to my feet and press my back against the wall, my eyes jumping around the small space. Maybe I'm safe, right here, for the moment. But I'm going to have to step carefully from now on.

Gradually the panic subsides; my pulse slows. I hear the surf and the screaming gulls and the ticking of my watch; I notice the ridged pattern on the metal stairway, outlined by dust and sand; I smell the rotten odor of the beach at low tide. I begin to think clearly again.

I can see why the duplicate might want to get rid of me. For the most part, having a duplicate is nothing but a pain. It's like a bad dream in which all the ordinary necessities of life—eating, wearing clothes, going to the bathroom, interacting with other people—are huge problems. Everything was so much easier and simpler before.

Everything would be so much better if one of us were gone.

But is death the only way to fix things? Wouldn't it be a million times better just to come out into the open, to announce our dual existence to the world and be twins? We both assumed from the beginning that secrecy was necessary. But is it important enough to kill for?

Now, for the first time, huddled against the dirty concrete wall, I try to imagine exactly what would happen if I presented the duplicate to Mom and Dad. They wouldn't want to believe it at first; Mom would be hysterical. But eventually they'd have to come to grips with the situation; they wouldn't have any choice. And then other people would find out. I'd be studied by scientists. I'd become a world celebrity, a hero—the first human being ever to duplicate himself. I'd go down in history!

No. The duplicate would never let that happen. He thinks he's me; he'd go on claiming to be me. And scientists would never be able to prove I'm the original, since their technology is so far behind that which produced the duplicate. What Dad told me about clones proves it. No one would ever know which was which. People would always wonder, always be suspicious of both of us. Everyone would be uncomfortable around us. I wouldn't be a celebrity, I'd be a freak.

And which one of us would Angela believe? I'd like to think she would somehow be able to tell that I'm the real David, but I already know she wouldn't—she believed the duplicate was me on Sunday night. There's no way the duplicate would ever back down and let her think I'm the original; he's too stubborn.

And what if she ended up believing in *him*? I groan. It makes me feel crazy even to think about that. Would *any* woman ever want to get married to me, and have kids, thinking I might be artificial, a kind of biological robot?

The best thing that could happen is that I'd spend the rest of my life as a freak, separated from everyone else in the world—separated from Angela—and tied to the duplicate, whom I'll never be able to trust.

How *can* I trust a creature that might have tried to kill me? A creature who lied so easily and behaved normally yesterday, knowing that today I'd probably have my head crushed by a concrete block? If that's true, the duplicate is a menace, a monster. No matter who I tell about him, that fact will never change. And how will they know which one to lock up, which one to protect? As long as the duplicate exists, I'll never have a moment of peace or safety again. I can't even take a step without thinking something's going to fall on my head.

Does that mean death really is the only solution?

I close my eyes. I want to give up. But how can I give up? I'm stuck in this. Maybe he's not trying to kill me. But he probably is. It's going to drive me nuts. It might even make me crazy enough to try to kill him first. I can't use the concrete block trick, he'll be prepared for that. But maybe there's some other way. . . .

"No! Stop it!"

My voice beats against the bare cement walls. I'm panicking all over again. I look at my watch, trying to think normally. It's six thirty. I've only been here a few minutes. It seems like so much longer. What am I going to do?

71

I pick up the bucket and the broom. I wait before starting up the stairs. We came down from the third floor fast last night, the duplicate running after me. There are no traps between here and the bedroom; the duplicate didn't have time to set anything up. But I still have trouble taking the first step. The second is a tiny bit easier. I stop to look around on almost every step, listening. It takes me a long time to get to the bedroom.

I sweep the sand and dirt and litter into a big pile, and dump it all into a plastic bag. Before I begin mopping, I have an idea. I carefully go downstairs. I stop in front of the second floor doorway and, just to make sure, push it all the way open again. I drag the concrete block into the dark room, far enough along the wall so that it can't be seen from the landing. I carefully set the door in exactly the same position it was in when the block was balanced on it.

Finally I'm doing something smart. If I just left the block where it fell, the duplicate would of course deny everything, and I'd learn nothing. But now I can test him. He said he'd come to the tower after school today. I'll ask him to check out the second floor. If he's the one who put the block there, he won't go through the door. If he didn't put the block there, he won't see any reason not to open it. This is better than balancing the block on top of the door, the way it was before. If I did that, it would fall on the duplicate only if he's innocent. If he's guilty, he just has to believe the block is still there, and he'll give himself away.

I mop the bedroom floor with cleaning fluid several times. I scrub out the sink, which doesn't do much good, since no water comes out of the tap. I find two chairs that still work and set them up at the table. Holding the bucket over my head, I very cautiously go up the stairs to the fourth floor. I push the door open with the broom handle and enter the observation room. This floor has the most windows—there's only one narrow one in the bedroom—and it's glaringly bright in here. There are a few pieces of uninteresting decrepit furniture, and a ladder leaning against one wall. I find several metal ashtrays, which I can use for candles in the bedroom. I also bring down a 1943 calendar, with a picture of a sexy woman in a funny two-piece bathing suit, and hang it on a nail in the bedroom wall.

It's nine thirty, almost time for Angela to get here. I still don't know what strategy to take with the duplicate. It's probably naive and dangerous to hope that the duplicate didn't set up the concrete block over the door, and maybe I should be constructing some traps of my own, if only for self-protection. But I just can't go around trying to kill or even hurt the duplicate until I'm sure he's guilty, and I won't know that until he comes back this afternoon.

And even if the duplicate *is* guilty, it will still be to my advantage if he thinks I don't suspect anything. Then he'll be less cautious, and more likely to walk blindly into any trap I might set up. If I arrange some trap now that doesn't work, it will only put the duplicate on guard. It makes more sense to play dumb until I know more—and that also allows me to put off making a decision.

Kissing Angela is wonderful. Just being with her, and successfully putting one over on the duplicate, gives me a feeling of confidence and control. Back in town we stop at my bank, and I take out fifty dollars, which almost cleans out my account. We eat hamburgers and fries; we hold hands in the movies when we're not eating popcorn and candy. Knowing we shouldn't be doing this and might be caught makes these stupid activities really exciting; we sneak around behind buildings and through back alleys, feeling like secret agents.

It's better with her than I expected, despite my preoccupation with the concrete block. In some funny way, knowing I almost got killed this morning makes me feel more relaxed with Angela. Whatever concerns I used to have are now trivial compared to what I have to face with the duplicate. My only disappointment is that I can't talk to her about the problem. I really want to get it off my chest, and several times I find myself on the verge of bringing it up. But I always stop.

I walk Angela almost to her house, and remind her not to tell anybody she was with me, and kiss her again. "You're a lot more fun than Carl," she whispers into my ear in a wonderfully intimate way. "Call me later."

At the hardware store, I buy an inexpensive alarm clock and the cheapest oil lamp they have, but it still uses up a lot of my cash. I head back to the beach. In the bedroom, I unpack the lamp and fill it with oil. The light really does make the little room more cozy, but I turn it off right away. Oil is expensive.

I pace in the observation room, looking at my watch, anticipating and at the same time dreading the duplicate's return. If the duplicate is innocent, he'll probably be furious about Angela. If he's guilty, he'll be wondering what happened to me—if not worrying about what to do with my corpse. It occurs to me that the duplicate is probably

74

even more anxious than I am. But so what if he is? He *deserves* to be worried.

The fourth floor has the best view, and every other minute I check the beach. When the tiny figure appears in the distance, I recognize the duplicate instantly. I squeeze my eyes shut for a moment, fighting panic again. I want to run away, to avoid this confrontation. But it can't be avoided.

I keep my eyes fixed on the duplicate as he approaches, hoping to see some indication of his state of mind. His walk is purposeful, his expression blank. When he reaches the bottom of the slope, I hurry down to the bedroom, as I've planned. I sit on the bed, chewing my lip and twisting my hands together. I hear the squeal of the outside door being opened and then carefully closed. I wait in the silence.

"Hey!" the duplicate calls, his voice hollow and uncertain from three floors below. "You up there?"

I say nothing. I listen. There are no footsteps. The duplicate is standing by the door, waiting to see if I answer him before approaching the second floor landing. It's what I guessed he might do, which is why I'm in the bedroom where I can pretend I've been asleep.

"Are you in there?" the duplicate calls again. Is there a frantic edge to his voice now?

I won't answer. I refuse to make it easy on him, to let him know right away that he has no grisly sight in store for him. Let him suffer a little longer.

And finally I hear footsteps—slow, careful footsteps—dull on the cement floor, pausing a moment, then percussive on the first metal step. Is the duplicate preparing himself for the sight of my crushed head? I quietly stretch out on the bed, wishing I could see the duplicate's reaction to the empty landing. But if I were waiting there to see what he does, it would be obvious that I know about the cement block, and it's vital to play dumb.

The duplicate's footsteps reach the second floor landing. The footsteps pause, but only briefly, just as if the duplicate hadn't been expecting to see anything there. But that is also part of the game. The duplicate doesn't want to tip me off that there is anything unusual about the landing, or the doorway.

Now I sit up in bed. "Who's there?" I call out. "Is that you?"

The footsteps move along the corridor. I stay on the bed. The duplicate appears in the doorway, holding a large paper bag. He watches me, an unreadable expression on his face, and says nothing.

I stretch and rub my eyes. "Oh, hi," I say. "I guess I fell asleep. I hardly slept at all last night, and I got up so early, and then I worked really hard today. See how I fixed up the—"

The duplicate throws the bag onto the table and leaps at me.

I'm totally unprepared. Before I know it, the duplicate has me pinned to the bed, his knees on my chest, one hand on my neck. He punches me on the head. "You jerk! You creep! You bastard!" he screams.

"Stop it! Leave me alone!" I yell back, trying to twist away from him.

"You were with Angela! Weren't you? I know you were!"

I cross my arms over my face. "So what if I was? That's not as bad as—" I shut up just in time.

"Not as bad as what?" He stops punching me, staring down at me.

"Not as bad as . . . as lying to me, and not telling me anything that really happened when you went over there." I keep my face turned away from him. "Get off me," I say, struggling to sit up.

He punches me again, grunting, then climbs off, his knee poking me in the ribs. "So I forgot to tell you a few things. You think that's worse than what you did—sneaking around and planning things behind my back? All sorts of people we know could mention to her that I was in school today, not just Carl. What's everybody going to think? And what are you going to tell her, jerk?"

I don't care what everybody thinks. I scramble off the bed before he has a chance to jump on me again. "What makes you so sure I was with her?"

"Don't give me that. You already admitted it. As soon as I found out she wasn't at school today, I knew she was meeting you. It's just the kind of sneaky thing you'd do."

"You knew it because you wanted to do the same thing. And you would have done it, if I was the one who went to school today."

"I would not," he says, "I'd never risk making everybody so suspicious. I'd never . . ." His eyes widen. "You didn't show her this place, did you?" The idea seems to terrify him.

"No. I'm not that dumb."

"Well, you're dumb enough." He sinks down into one of the chairs at the table, still not saying anything about all the work I've done. "What are we going to do? What if she tells other people? How are we ever going to explain to her *this* time about being in two places at once, for a whole day?"

"Maybe nobody will say anything," I mumble. It's hard for me to get as worked up about this problem as he seems to be, since I'm worrying about the cement block. How am I going to find out if he'll go through that door?

"You *did* make her promise not to tell anybody she was with you, no matter what, didn't you?"

"Of course I did."

"So, if we're lucky, then Angela will be the only one who knows about us," the duplicate says slowly.

I sit down across from him, leaning forward. "But she can't know; nobody can."

"You don't want her to know because you're afraid that if she does, she'll like me better than you," he says, looking hard at me.

"That won't worry me," I tell him. "Not after today."

He grabs my arm and squeezes it. "What happened today? Tell me everything."

I laugh, pulling my arm away. "Like you told me everything that happened the night you went over to her house?"

"Look, we've got to stop this," he says, sounding worried, not angry any more. "We've got to trust each other. It's the only way we'll get through this."

Trust each other? He expects me to fall for that, after he tried to kill me? But I play along, wanting him to think I don't know about the concrete block. "You're right. I'll tell you everything—if you *promise* you'll tell me everything too, from now on."

"Okay. I'll tell you everything. And I'm sorry about the other night. I just wasn't used to the situation then. I'll never be that forgetful again. I promise." He reaches out his hand to shake on it.

Of course, he's just promising as a way of persuading me to tell him everything that happened with Angela today. I promise anyway, and shake on it. Why not? It's only words. And I do tell him most of what happened, though I leave out the part about kissing her.

"Well, I just hope she doesn't tell anybody," he says, when I finish. "And I guess it's *possible* that nobody will

79

mention to her that I was in school today. But if some-body does, and she asks you about it at school tomorrow, I guess you'll just have to tell her the truth." He sighs and looks away from me. "I don't know what else we can do; she'll have to have an explanation. And maybe it won't be so bad if she finds out." He turns back to me. "But if you do have to tell her about us, then bring her back here after school. You have to give me a chance to explain things to her too. It's only fair."

I'm not concerned with what's fair anymore. And I can't think as far ahead as tomorrow; I have more immediate concerns. "Sure, if I have to tell her, I'll bring her over here tomorrow," I say, just so he'll shut up about it. "Hey, did you see the lamp I bought? Look how I fixed the place up."

He admires the lamp, and asks how much it cost, and I light it—it's already getting dark in here. And now, finally, he tells me that the room looks nice; he even laughs at the calendar. "You want to stay here tonight?" he asks me.

I glare at him. "Do you?"

"Maybe."

"Oh, come off it."

He turns back to the calendar. "So, did you explore the rest of the place?" he says casually.

"I went up to the top floor. There's a lot of windows up there, but that's about it."

"You didn't look around anywhere else?"

"No. I was pretty busy in here." I pause; then I make myself say it. "You want to check the rest of the place out now?"

"Sure. Why not?"

I follow him. He doesn't walk real fast, but he's not creeping around as if he expects a booby trap of mine to fall on him either. On the stairway, he goes up. I stifle the impulse to tell him to go down, not wanting to make him suspicious. We look around the fourth floor. Even with all the windows, it's getting dark up here now too. He examines the ladder carefully, and I wonder if he's trying to figure out a way to use it in another trap for me.

"Seems to be pretty sturdy," he says.

"Good. We can use it when we paint the ceilings."

"You don't have to be sarcastic," he whines. "A ladder could come in handy."

I'll bet it could, I say to myself.

"Well, I guess that's everything," he says, starting down the stairs.

Now I can't hold it in. "What about the second floor? I never went in there."

"Oh, that's right. Funny, I forgot about it."

Sure he did.

It's almost completely dark on the third floor. "We need the flashlight," I say, and quickly get it from the bedroom. We go down to the second floor landing. I pause by the door, not knowing how to get him to go through first. I look away from the door for a moment, not wanting to seem too eager. Then I notice something, and shine the flashlight on the landing wall. "Hey, look at this," I tell him.

Scrawled on the wall, in sloppy black letters, are the words: *Life is hard. Then you die.*

The duplicate says nothing.

"But don't you think this is weird?" I say, feeling a chill. "It wasn't there this morning. And it looks like our handwriting."

"Well, I didn't write it," he says defensively. "It must have been here all along, and you just never noticed it."

"You could have done it just now, on your way up," I tell him. I know he didn't pause for long on the landing, but when else could he have done it?

"I told you, I didn't do it."

"Don't lie to me."

"I'm not," he insists. "It's been there all along."

"I thought we were going to tell each other everything," I remind him. "I thought we promised."

"I'm not lying. I didn't write it." He slaps the wall. "*I* don't think it looks so much like our handwriting. It's printed. Somebody wrote it there years ago—maybe that crazy murderer did it—and you just didn't notice it until now. I saw it the first day."

"You are lying. And it *does* look like our handwriting." Why won't he admit that he wrote it?

"You're just being paranoid," he says, as stubborn as ever.

But I have a right to be paranoid. Now more than ever, I've got to find out if he knows about the concrete block. "Oh, forget it. Come on, let's see what's in there," I urge him.

He takes the flashlight, steps past me, and shines the beam through the slightly open doorway. He pushes the door open with his foot.

I hear the scraping sound, hardly believing it. "Look out!" I scream, pulling him back by his shoulders.

82

The concrete block, which has been carefully reposi-
tioned, misses him.

We both stare at it for a moment in the flashlight beam.
Then he turns on me. "You put that there," he says, half
choking, out of breath. "You tried to make me go through
that door. You tried to *kill* me!"

"No. I didn't put it there, I swear I didn't." I grab his
shoulders again. "You have to believe me!"

"Why should I?" he screams at me.

He seems genuinely upset. Is it possible that he really
didn't put it there yesterday? I break down and tell him
the truth. "Because the same thing happened to me when
I came in this morning. I opened the door, and it fell
down and almost killed me. I was pretty sure you did it.
You were here all day yesterday. So I hid it, to see if
you'd walk through the door. I *didn't* put it back, just in
case you were innocent."

He pulls away from my hands. "Sure, sure, that makes
all the sense in the world," he says. But his sarcasm isn't
convincing. His mood has suddenly changed. He's not
angry anymore; he seems confused, as if he can't take it
all in. His eyes slide away from my face. "I . . . you're
crazy if you expect me to believe you. You must have
put it there, because . . . because I didn't."

"Then why didn't you just walk through the door?" I
ask him. "You stood back and kicked it open. That proves
you knew it was there."

"I just didn't want to go barging into a dark room,
that's all. I didn't put it there, I . . . I swear it," he mur-
murs, his voice fading. He chews on his lip, his eyes looking past me as though I'm not there.

I can't figure him out. "I don't believe you," I say.

He looks quickly back at me, and down. "I didn't do it, that's all," he whispers.

But he could easily be lying to me. He could have put it there yesterday, and now I'll never know. "Well, if you didn't put it there—and I have no reason to believe you didn't—then somebody else must have, before we even found this place. Because I didn't do it." It's the truth; I didn't put it there. And he'll probably never believe me either.

But he surprises me. "Yes, that must be it," he says eagerly, nodding. "Somebody else must have put it there, that same homicidal maniac, before we ever came here."

I sigh. Why is he pretending to believe me? Why is he suddenly so distracted? "I'm getting out of here," I say, pulling the flashlight from his limp grasp and moving toward the stairs to the first floor. "Well, come on. What are you waiting for?"

"Leave me the flashlight," he says slowly. "I'll . . . spend the night here."

"What?" I spin around, terrified and amazed. "You're going to stay here all night, alone?" I'm almost as upset as if he were trying to make me do it.

"I already told you I might want to. I guess it's because of how . . . you fixed it up. I'm kind of getting to feel comfortable here."

"That *proves* you set that trap for me," I say. "Otherwise you'd be too scared to stay here. It just doesn't make any sense. Why are you doing this? What if something happens to you? Come on. We'll be late."

"What do you mean it doesn't make any sense?" he asks me, coming out of his daze and beginning to sound sure of himself again. "It makes all the sense in the world. That's why I found this place, isn't it? So we wouldn't run into trouble at home. Well, now I think I can stand it, so why shouldn't I try it? I picked up plenty of good stuff to eat at the deli, enough for the morning too. And if I get scared—well, check behind the garage at nine o'clock. I'll be there if I decide I want to come home. Then you can sneak me inside."

I stand there staring at him, the flashlight hanging in my hand making an oval pool of light on the dirty floor between us. "You know," I say at last. "I think you really mean it."

"I just feel like I want to try it, that's all." He reaches for the flashlight. "Look for me behind the garage to-morrow morning before you go to school. And don't forget to go out there at nine tonight too, in case I back down."

"Yeah. See you at nine," I say dryly, trying to get the last word in, trying not to feel like the cowardly one. I turn and walk down the stairs.

Supper is the first decent meal I've had in two days, but I barely have an appetite. It bothers me more than I would have expected that the duplicate is staying by him-self at the tower. In one way, it doesn't make any sense for me to be upset about it, since it's so much easier and more comfortable to be at home without him, not having to worry about getting caught.

But I can't shake the feeling that he has some ulterior motive for staying at the tower—it would take a lot to get *me* to stay there alone. I keep assuring myself that he'll be out at the garage at nine. I tell Mom and Dad I'm going for a walk, and they exchange significant glances—they think I'm going out to moon about Angela.

The duplicate isn't there. I'm disappointed and I'm worried—not because I miss him, but because I don't trust him. I wait outside until nine thirty, thinking about his strange behavior this afternoon and trying to figure out what he's up to. Finally I give up and go back to my room. As I'm getting undressed, I happen to glance over at the aquarium. At first I can see only one fish, swimming frantically back and forth. I step closer, suddenly afraid.

And then I see the other fish lying motionless in the sand at the bottom of the tank.

11

The fish that's still alive has a black mark like a ribbon behind his gills, and a triangular one on his right fin. His mouth is open, exposing the two rows of razor-sharp teeth. As he swims, both his upper and lower teeth push out beyond his mouth, then sink back, push out and sink back, never stopping, his face stretching and shrinking with each relentless extension and retraction of his jaws.

I want to get the dead fish out of there, so he won't pollute the water and also to see whether or not he died of wounds—his body is partly covered by sand. But as soon as my hand breaks the surface of the water, the living fish flashes toward it, teeth extended to the limit, and I barely get my hand away fast enough to avoid being bitten. The fish begins obsessively batting his hideous, demented little face against the glass.

Is this one the duplicate or the original? Neither fish had the black marks when I first duplicated the original; it took a day or so for the marks to show up. Do they appear on the original because some of his cells have been used to make the duplicate? Or do they appear on the duplicate because he is an artificial creation? And what does this mean in terms of my duplicate and me?

There is one thing I can find out. I pull off my clothes and study my right arm, my right leg, the entire right side of my body. There are no unusual markings. I get a hand mirror and look carefully at the back of my neck in the mirror on the closet door. I can find nothing that wasn't there before. All I can see is how pale and tired I look.

I sit down and stare dumbly at the crazy fish, trying to think logically. If the dead fish was murdered by the fish with the markings, who seems to have become a maniac, then I may be in serious danger from the duplicate. And if the unmarked fish was not murdered, but somehow died automatically because of being involved in the duplication process, then I am really doomed.

What I need to do is check out the duplicate tomorrow to see if he has any marks on him. If he doesn't, that could mean the process takes longer in human beings. In that case, I still might develop the markings, and then lose my mind and end up bashing my head against walls. So might he—after killing me first. My only hope is that duplication might be different for fish than for human beings, and none of these things will happen to me. But that doesn't seem logical at all.

I get in bed and turn out the light, sick of thinking about it. But naturally I hardly sleep at all. In the morning I feel worse than ever, fuzzy headed and disoriented. I wonder if I might be going crazy already, and check my body again. I still don't find any marks. My dark blond hair is lank and greasy in the mirror, and my face looks terrible, pale and puffy, with dark rings under my eyes.

I'm going to have to figure out how to check out the duplicate, to see if he has marks, without making him wonder what I'm doing. I don't want to tell him about the fish, at least not until I understand it better. I can't trust him. No matter what he *said* yesterday, the most sensible interpretation of the facts is that he put the concrete block there and tried to kill me. That means he is my deadly enemy. If I can learn something about the fish that relates to us, something he doesn't know, then I might be able to use it to protect myself.

After breakfast, during which Mom and Dad keep looking at me strangely (or am I only imagining it?), I think of something as I'm putting on my gloves. I don't have much time, but this is important. I run upstairs and, with my leather jacket and gloves on, I reach into the aquarium. The fish goes berserk, sinking his teeth into the glove and thrashing wildly. I try to ignore it, and manage to get my fingers around the dead fish and lift it. The crazy fish clings to the glove, convulsing as I pull my hand out of the water—he'd rather die than let go of me. Cursing, I finally shake him off. He instantly leaps back out of the water, jaws snapping, and almost gets the glove again. Is that what one of us is going to turn into?

I study the dead fish—what's left of him. Part of the skin of his face remains, but the rest of him is hardly more than a skeleton. In the bathroom, I flush him down the toilet, feeling sicker than ever. As I hurry down the stairs, I realize that I haven't really learned anything. It's possible that the marked fish killed him by tearing him to shreds. But it's also possible that he died for some other reason, and the crazy one didn't start eating him until he was already a corpse. I still don't know what any of it means.

But I do have an idea. I get what I need from Mom's studio. I'm not really sure how I'm going to use it, but I figure I might as well be prepared. I start to put the stuff into my inside jacket pocket. Then I think better of it, and button it into the big patch pocket on my pants.

The duplicate is waiting out behind the garage. He looks a little tired, but not nearly as bad as I looked in the mirror. He doesn't have dark rings under his eyes, his hair is thick and wavy, and it even seems lighter in color than mine, though that must be because he's standing in the sunlight. He doesn't say anything as he turns toward me, his eyes wide, his red lips parted slightly. He seems strangely shy. I don't know what to make of it.

"So you survived the night," I say, not very enthusiastically.

"Yeah. You steal anything for me to eat? I'm starving to death."

"How could I steal anything? You've got the backpack. And you told me you had plenty of good stuff from the deli, enough for the morning too."

"Oh." He blinks. "Well, that's right, I did. But it didn't . . . turn out to be as much as I thought."

What's the matter with him? What kind of act is he pulling now? "Well, you can't blame me after you told me you had all that food," I say. "So, did you have a nice cozy time there?"

"No, not particularly. It wasn't as bad as I thought,

but I still almost gave up and came back at nine. It was really boring and uncomfortable . . . and scary too," he adds, looking away from me. "But then, I just didn't want to admit to you that I couldn't do it. So I stayed."

"I'm impressed." It's true, though I don't enjoy admitting it. "Let me have the backpack; I'm going to be late for school," I say, stepping around behind him and reaching for it, hoping to get a good look at the back of his neck.

But he turns around to face me before I can see anything. "Wait . . . just a minute," he says hesitantly. "Remember, on Monday, I did that favor for you, going to band practice? And . . . and you said you'd do the same kind of thing for me some day?"

"Yeah, what about it?" I say, irritated by his manner as well as by the way he's preventing me from seeing his neck.

"Well, I know it's a lot to ask, but there's a practical reason for it. . . ." He looks away and sighs, chewing on his lip. "See, I never had a chance to tell you what happened at school yesterday, what I said to everybody. And there's no time to tell you now. So, you'll probably make lots of mistakes, and *everybody* will start thinking we're peculiar. Unless . . . Well, um, do you think you could possibly, I mean, maybe could you let me go to school today, even though I went yesterday? You said you'd . . . return the favor. And then I'll tell you *everything* that happens, and you can go tomorrow."

"Huh?" I stare at him. It's not his request that's so peculiar, it's the way he's making it, forcing the words out so timidly. What's he afraid of? "Oh, I get it. You want to be there with Angela, in case she suspects anything, so you can get her on your side first." I snort. "Come on, give me the backpack." I step around behind him again and fumble with the pack, purposely getting one of the straps caught on his shirt collar.

He sighs, and shrugs his shoulders, but this time he doesn't turn around, talking with his back to me, his head down. "I know that's what it sounds like, but that isn't really it. It's for the reason I said. And also, I just feel so . . . funny, after spending the night in the tower. It was so strange and kind of eerie. I need to do something really normal and ordinary so I won't feel so . . . so outside of things. And I promise, if Angela suspects something, if I have to tell her, I'll bring her back to the tower after school, so we can both talk to her," he goes on earnestly, his voice a little hoarse.

I pull down his shirt collar. There is a thick black line like a ribbon on the back of his neck. I whip my hands away, letting go of the pack.

He turns to face me, not meeting my eyes. "I'd . . . I'd really appreciate it," he says miserably. "I'd do anything you want in return. So, could you . . . please let me go? Just this once?"

In a way, I was hoping to find the mark. But now that I've seen it, I'm shocked. Does this mean he's going to go insane like the fish? Suddenly I feel sorry for him. Maybe I should let him go to school; it might be his last chance before his mind goes.

But I can't let him know I pity him; I can't give anything away. I try to respond normally. "Well, if it's not because of Angela, then it's because you set up another trap at the tower and you want me to walk into it. You expect me to fall for *that*?"

"No, no. I promise I didn't set up a trap. I mean it." He's staring directly at me now, his eyes glistening. The most peculiar thing about it is that somehow I get the feeling that he's feeling sorry for *me*. But that makes no sense at all. Maybe he's already going crazy. "You don't have to go back to the tower if you think there's a trap. Don't go back there—wait somewhere else until I come back from school and we'll go together," he says hopefully. Then his voice returns to a monotone. "But please let me go to school."

"All right then, go!" I say. "Just go if it means so much to you. But I won't forget this. You have to promise to let me spend the next two days with Angela. Okay? Is it a promise?"

He nods mutely, as though he can't trust himself to speak.

"Cheer up, you're getting what you want, aren't you? And good luck." I reach out and grab his right hand to shake it encouragingly. On the back of it, there is a black triangle about an inch across. I drop it quickly. "Better get going, you're already late."

The school and the beach are in opposite directions. Every time I look back at him as we walk away from each other, he's looking back at me.

I keep wondering, as I walk along the beach, if I'm letting him get away with something. But he seemed so genuine, and so unhappy. It's hard for me to believe it was all an act. I try to force myself to think rationally, going over his behavior at the tower yesterday. I'd love

93

to believe he didn't put the cement block there, that some unknown person did it. But is that logical? Doesn't all the evidence point to him?

I stop outside the back of the tower. What am I doing here? Why am I even considering going inside? I've walked to the tower almost automatically. But if some nut really did replace the block yesterday, then I'm crazy to go in.

The plywood is in place over the door. That means no one is inside. And the duplicate did survive the night here. Maybe it's not so dangerous; maybe there is some other explanation. I'll never find out what it is if I don't check it out. I have to go in. I push down the plywood, kick open the door and jump out of the way.

Nothing happens. I know nobody can be in here, since it is impossible to replace the plywood from the inside. All I have to be afraid of are things falling on me. There's nothing over this door. I step inside.

It takes me a while to get to the stairs. It takes me even longer to get up the stairs, creeping along the wall with my hands over my head. If I didn't know for a fact that nobody could possibly be inside, I wouldn't be able to do any of this. I keep telling myself that I just want to see the room after the duplicate spent the night there. Maybe I'll find an answer to something.

Outside the bedroom door I notice, just before I step on it, a drawing scratched in the grit on the corridor floor. It's like a simple child's drawing of a bare assymetrical tree—a line about a foot long that splits into a fork. The right fork continues on for another foot; the left fork splits into two lines again after six inches. It actually looks more like an ugly claw than a tree. Shivering, I peer cautiously into the bedroom.

The duplicate did pick up a lot of food at the deli. The table is littered with paper cartons and soft drink cans and greasy plastic utensils. I'm surprised he's such a slob; in fact, I resent it, after I worked so hard to clean the place up. I step quickly into the room to throw the stuff into the garbage bag.

The bed creaks. I cry out, jumping back, my heart going crazy.

Someone sits up on the bed. Someone wearing the old sweat clothes I couldn't find at home the other day. Someone who looks a whole lot like me.

"Took you long enough," he says, stretching his hands above his head and yawning.

12

He gets up and moves toward me, smiling sleepily, pushing back his curly tousled hair. He's wearing the maroon sweat shirt with the faded, ferocious white bear on it. The old elastic on my gray sweat pants is so loose that they're slipping off his waist. The stuffing is leaking out of the ancient blue running shoes.

I back away from him, feeling for the door behind me.

He laughs pleasantly. "No, no, don't go, you just got here." He gestures at a chair. "Sit down. Make yourself comfortable."

I remain in the doorway, not moving any closer. "When did he generate *you*?" I ask him, trying not to sound as frightened as I must seem.

"You mean when did *I* generate him, don't you?" says Duplicate B. "And the word for it, by the way, is *bifurcate*, to split in two. You saw the bifurcation diagram out there." He slouches into a chair, casually pushes some trash off the table onto the floor, and leans forward on his elbows. "Today's Wednesday, isn't it? Oh, I bifurcated a while ago, the day I found this place and brought the Spee-Dee-Dupe here. Monday I guess it was. I've been hanging around here all this time. And it took you this long to find out." He smiles and shakes his head at me. "I'm surprised you didn't guess before this. There were so many clues."

Now I know why the other duplicate seemed so confused yesterday afternoon. He really didn't know anything about the concrete block. This duplicate put it there, this duplicate replaced it, and this duplicate wrote *Life is hard. Then you die* on the wall beside the door.

I also know for sure that I've never seen this duplicate before. I've begun to notice that Duplicate A, the one I'm familiar with, seems to look a little different from me. This one looks slightly different from both of us, his hair light blond and very curly, his face narrow and almost elfin, with large eyes and delicate features and absolutely flawless skin. What does that mean about the Spee-Dee-Dupe?

"Of course, Monday was the second time I bifurcated," he goes on. "The first time was on Sunday, the day I found the Spee-Dee-Dupe at the beach. That's when I bifurcated to make you."

I'm not surprised this one thinks he's the original. What I *do* find hard to believe is that Duplicate A was idiotic enough to bifurcate. Suddenly I'm furious at him. How could he do this, knowing how difficult it was to have only *one* duplicate around? What's it going to be like with two of them? I begin to panic. What's going to happen now? I can't trust either of them. How am I ever going to get out of this? I just want to run away and forget the whole thing.

But I can't. I have to deal with it. I struggle to stay calm. But I'm more scared than ever. It's going to turn into a two-against-one situation now. In fact, the two of them probably have *already* been plotting against me. That's why Duplicate A bifurcated, to have someone on his side. How am I going to get through this?

"Well? Aren't you going to sit down?" says Duplicate B. "I don't bite."

I remember the extending and retracting jaws of the fish. And suddenly I can't keep myself from saying, "You may not bite, but you drop concrete blocks on people's heads. You put that block up there, and you knew *I* was coming here yesterday morning."

He chuckles. "Don't flatter yourself. I wasn't sure which one of you would be going through that door first. You could have changed places, like you did today. But now I'm glad that you didn't get hurt."

"Yeah? But you *did* try to kill one of us," I say, my voice rising. "And when it didn't work the first time, you put it back. How could you *do* that?"

He laughs again. "Don't give me that holier-than-thou crap," he says cheerfully. "You know you want him out of the way too. You would have ended up doing the same thing eventually. I just figured it was time to get the ball rolling."

And I used to think Duplicate A was bad! Compared to this monster, he's an angel. "No wonder he was so upset today," I say, not thinking. "Who wouldn't be, after being here with you all night long!"

"Don't waste your pity on him," says Duplicate B, looking up at me with wide-eyed innocence. "Did he tell you about me when he sent you back here? Did he warn you that I'd be here?"

No, he didn't. And Duplicate B is reminding me of that to make me think I can trust only him, that he's on my side. But he's not. As confused as I am, I can't let myself forget that that the two of them are probably plotting against me. They bifurcated, and now they're allies and I'm the enemy. Again, I fight down my panic. Duplicate B mustn't realize I know what's going on. I have to pretend I believe he's on my side and play along for now.

"I hope you're not going to be upset that he betrayed you. Please don't feel bad," Duplicate B says kindly. "Really, he's not worth it. And don't worry about what he's saying to Angela right this minute. She won't—"

I step quickly toward him. "Angela! What do you mean? Did he tell you what he was going to say to Angela today? Is he trying to turn her against me? Is *that* why he wanted to go to school? Tell me!"

The smile leaves Duplicate B's face. His voice turns cold. "Oh, Angela this, Angela that!" he says mockingly. "I hope you're not going to be as boring about her as he is."

"You know how I feel about Angela. What was he going to say to her today? Does he want to take her away from me? You have to tell me!"

Duplicate B looks disgusted. "See what I mean? That girl makes you stupid. Think, man. How can he take her away from you? She thinks he *is* you."

"Oh. Oh, that's right," I say, feeling like an idiot.

"On the other hand, he's such a sap it wouldn't surprise me if he *did* turn her against all of us just by being himself. Not that it would matter. That girl's trouble, believe me."

If Duplicate B thinks Angela's trouble, what does he think *he* is? His attitude toward Angela is one of the strangest things about him. He really seems to hate her. I don't understand it; I don't understand how he can be so casually brutal. Why is he so different from me and Duplicate A when three days ago we were the same person? How can he possibly hate Angela while we're so crazy about her? "What don't you like about her?" I ask him.

"She's using us, can't you see that?" he says, as though it's an obvious fact. "She's just pretending to like us to make that dumb jock boyfriend of hers jealous. Didn't you realize that at her house on Sunday night?"

"I wasn't there on Sunday night, remember?"

"Oh, that's right. No wonder . . ."

"What do you mean? What happened?"

He purses his lips, thinking. "Well, as soon as we finshed the math she got restless, bored. She called up Carl and stayed on the phone with him *forever*—I had to sit there listening to her dull, preachy brother. And when she finally got off the phone she hardly noticed I was there. And then her brother kept talking about what a great guy Carl was, and she kept nodding and agreeing. It was humiliating. She kept looking at the clock, as though she could hardly wait for me to get out of there so she could call him back. Then, when I was coming out of the bathroom, I overheard her saying something to her brother about how the evening wasn't a total waste, because of the math problems." He rolls his eyes. "No brains, and she's not even very attractive, if you ask me."

At least this duplicate tells me things. The trouble is, they're all bad. What he's saying about Angela is almost too much to take. But is he really telling me the truth? "But yesterday she . . ." I start to argue with him. I want to tell him how great it was with her, how much she seemed to be enjoying herself, how long we kissed, how she told me I was much more interesting than Carl. But I stop myself. If I tell him, he'll just turn it around and make it sound ugly and use it as ammunition against her. I'm beginning to learn how to deal with Duplicate B.

"What about yesterday?" he wants to know.

"Nothing. She just didn't seem bored, that's all."

"Yeah, yesterday. Why didn't you bring her in here?" he reprimands me. "I figured that's why you arranged to meet her, so you could take her into the bedroom and get her to express her gratitude to you for *me* doing her math problems. I was looking forward to dropping something on her. The concrete block was really meant for her, you know."

I swear to myself that I will never, no matter what, let Angela get anywhere near this guy. "Oh, come off it," I say. "You expect me to believe that? You're just talking big. You'd never kill Angela. It's not like killing one of us. That wouldn't be so risky, since nobody knows we even exist, so nobody would miss us or even . . . notice that anything had . . . happened." My voice trails away as I realize what I'm saying.

Duplicate B is smiling at me again. "Yeah, interesting situation we're in, isn't it?" he says, his voice brimming with warmth and enthusiasm. "Nobody would ever notice. That solves about ninety percent of the problems of killing somebody, doesn't it? It would really be a shame not to take advantage of that fact; we'd just be throwing away this fantastic opportunity, don't you think?"

The expression on his face is so infectiously playful that I actually find myself smiling back at him. His jolly manner is hard to resist, even though I'm horrified by what he's saying. "I guess you could look at it that way," I say, grinning helplessly, feeling like a fool but unable to control my facial muscles.

"You really *are* a lot more fun than the other one!" he exclaims joyfully, leaning across the table and slapping me on the back. "It really makes me happy to know you and I can get along after all." He relaxes back in his chair. "Now I wish I'd never bifurcated the second time. Three is just too many. But there's a solution to that problem. And we'd better start setting it up."

"Start setting what up?" I say.

"The death trap for the other one. Together we should be able to come up with something really foolproof and clever."

"Oh, yeah. Fantastic," I say numbly.

"What's the matter? Nothing's the matter, is it?" he asks me, his eyes full of concern.

"No, no, everything's *fine*. I'm just kind of wiped out, that's all. I can't remember the last time I had a good night's sleep."

"Me too. We hardly slept at all last night, either," he

says. "But we don't have time to relax now. We've got to get rid of *him* first. He'll only make trouble for us. So, you got any bright ideas about how to kill him?"

Now I'm more confused than ever. Duplicate B really seems to be serious about killing Duplicate A. Does that mean they *haven't* been plotting against me after all? If they haven't, maybe I can really trust Duplicate A. Duplicate B could have forced him to send me to the tower today—he seemed pretty miserable about doing it. And Duplicate B is obviously the monstrous one. If Duplicate A and I could somehow work together, then maybe we can get the better of him. That's probably my only chance.

Except for one little problem: How can I work together with Duplicate A if we're about to kill him?

13

If only I could get out of here and find Duplicate A!
But Duplicate B will never let me go, because he knows
what I might do. There's nothing to stop him from killing me to keep me from getting away from him. So what
am I going to do?

Then I remember the idea I had at home this morning.
A crazy plan occurs to me. There's not much chance I'll
be able to get away with this one either. Duplicate B isn't
gullible, and he's similar enough to me that he may be
able to see through any lies I tell him. But I don't know
what else to do. Even if he doesn't fall for it, the situation
couldn't get much worse.

"Well?" Duplicate B says, less pleasantly. "Come on,
give me some ideas, help me brainstorm. What's the point
of keeping you around if you're not going to make things
easier for me?"

"Okay, okay. I'm thinking. But I have to go to the
bathroom." I stand up. "Think we have enough time for
me to do that?"

He laughs, also standing up. "Sure. But don't waste my time trying to get away. You *know* I'd never let you do that." He grins and pinches my cheek hard, using his fingernails, squeezing the flesh for a long moment. Then he lets go and marches out into the corridor. He stands with his feet planted on either side of the bifurcation diagram, blocking the way to the stairs. He folds his arms across his chest and gestures sharply with his head. "Get going," he orders me. "I'll be waiting right here in case you try to make a run for it."

I trudge off to the bathroom at the end of the corridor. As soon as I get the door closed, I pull out the brush, tube of paint and piece of paper I took from Mom's studio this morning. But I don't have time to practice on the paper and quickly put it back. It's not easy to paint the back of my neck, especially since there's no mirror in here and I have to hurry. But I take the time to try to make the mark on the back of my right hand look as much as possible like the one I saw on Duplicate A—except a lot bigger. I really do have to go to the toilet, and I try to be as noisy about it as possible. It's pretty disgusting in here, since the pipes must have frozen years ago and Duplicate B has been using the bathroom for the last three days.

"Took you long enough," Duplicate B says, still standing where I left him. He doesn't move until I go back into the bedroom.

"I do some of my best thinking on the toilet," I tell him. "Maybe we could rig up something with the ladder." I sit down at the table. Of course I say nothing about the fish right now; if I did, he'd connect the marks with my trip to the bathroom. I'm going to have to wait

105

for just the right moment. I also want to wait until I can see if *he* has any marks. I can use the time to think; my story is going to have to be pretty convincing.

"Yeah, I was thinking about the ladder too," says Duplicate B, sitting down across from me. Unfortunately, the sweat shirt he's wearing has extremely long sleeves that cover the backs of his hands.

"Like maybe sawing one of the rungs almost all the way through," I suggest. "And then getting him to climb up on it, maybe over the stairs so he'll fall farther."

"No good. What are we going to saw it with? And do you really think he'd climb up on it if one of us suggested it?" He smiles tightly at me. "You're not taking this seriously. You're just saying anything to try to appease me. You're going to have to do better than that."

"Well, what do you expect? I'm not used to thinking about things like this! And I don't want to kill him anyway. I hate the whole idea of it! There must be some other way."

"Oh, come on, pull yourself together, be reasonable," he says with total self-assurance, as though it's irrational of me *not* to want to kill somebody.

That gives me another idea. "But I just don't know if I can stand it, it scares me so much," I say, looking down and shaking my head. "It just makes me feel so crazy and kind of . . . disoriented. There's *got* to be another way." I look up at him again, opening my eyes wide, pulling at my hair, trying to act crazy like the fish. "Couldn't we just come out of hiding and tell everybody!" I say wildly, even though I've already decided that's not a possibility.

"What's the matter with you?" he says, taken aback.

106

For the first time, he actually seems a little frightened. "Don't you know what would happen if we did that? It would ruin everything, for the rest of our lives. We'd never have another moment of peace or privacy again; they'd never leave us alone. We'd never get away with anything after that."

"Well, then couldn't we just go on like we are?" I mumble, knowing that's equally impossible.

"And spend the rest of our lives hiding like this? And the two of you driving yourselves crazy about Angela? No way," he says firmly.

"Yeah, but why should I help you get rid of him, if you're just going to turn around and kill me as soon as he's out of the way?" I ask him, wondering how he's going to get out of this one, wishing he'd push his sleeves back.

"Just because three is too many doesn't mean we can't get away with having two of us," he says, as though he means it. "You know what the advantages are; you think you're the original too, so you remember why you bifurcated. Not to mention, having you around gives me a lot of freedom to take risks. If I do something really wild, and it backfires, then *you* can be the one who gets blamed for it and gets caught, you can be the scapegoat— and I'll just fade conveniently out of the picture." He sits back in his chair and smiles at me, pushing back his sleeves and folding his hands together. But his right hand is hidden by a soft drink can, so I can't see if it's marked or not.

"You're telling me you'd do that to me, and you expect me to help you?"

"It's better than dying, isn't it?" He leans forward sud-

107

denly and bangs his fist on the table. "Because those are the alternatives. So you better hurry up and prove you'll be an asset, not a liability. Otherwise I'll get rid of *both* of you and just bifurcate again."

"Okay, okay," I say, really trying to come up with something he'll like now. "Maybe . . . maybe the ladder could fall on *him*."

"Be serious. That wouldn't hurt him enough."

"Well, but what if it happened when he's coming up the stairs or something."

He considers it, his expression blank. Then he nods with approval. "Hey, maybe you've got something there," he says, pleased and excited again. "If he was knocked backwards down a whole flight, with the ladder banging down on top of him—and maybe the concrete block thrown in too, for insurance—he might snap his spinal cord or get a concussion. Even if that didn't happen, he'd probably break *something*." He's beaming at me now. "Not bad at all. I'm impressed. Maybe you've got a chance. Now we've got to figure out the details, like how to set it up so he'll trip it when he's coming up the stairs."

"Does it have to be so complicated?"

"Yes. It has to happen automatically; that's the fun part. Now let's see . . ." He leans forward, his elbows on the table, and rests his chin on his two clasped hands. But his left hand, unmarked, is covering the back of his right hand. I feel like grabbing his hands and getting a good look, though I know that would also be too obvious. Why won't he just let me see his hand?

We set up the trap together. It's Duplicate B who comes up with the clever details: the drawing of the skull and

108

crossbones on the landing to distract Duplicate A so he won't notice the rope hanging down from the ladder until the right moment; the puddle of oil on the step underneath the rope, so that he'll slip and flail his arms for balance and grab the rope without thinking; the ladder, supported by a chair, balanced on the railing above, with the concrete block in the middle of it to come sliding down on him along with the ladder. Duplicate B tests the balance and weights of things a lot; he is a perfectionist. As we work, I keep trying to get a look at the back of his neck or hand, but never manage to do it.

I realize now that I can't just tell him about the marks. The story will be a lot more convincing if I pretend I'm trying to hide it from him, and he has to pry it out of me. I keep trying to get him to notice the mark on my hand, practically waving it in his face. But he's too preoccupied with setting up the trap to notice anything. Once we've finished, Duplicate B is full of eager anticipation, impatient for Duplicate A to show up so he can see how it's going to work. I wish I didn't have to be there.

Waiting, up in the bedroom again, I know my time is running out. School is over; Duplicate A could get here at any moment. Even if Duplicate B doesn't have any marks himself—whatever that might mean—he'll see them soon enough on Duplicate A, and that ought to prove to him that mine are real.

But Duplicate B is standing by the window, scanning the beach for Duplicate A, paying no attention to me. I clean up a little, throwing all the trash into the garbage bag. How can I get him to notice the marks?

He turns to me. "What time is it now?" he says, not

wanting to leave his vantage point even long enough to look at the alarm clock.

Luckily, I happen to be near the window at the moment he asks. I hold the wristwatch on my right hand up to him, hoping the mark will stand out in the light from outside.

"Thanks. What you got on your hand?" he says without interest, turning to look back out the window.

"Oh, my hand?" I say, whipping it away from him. "Uh . . . nothing. Nothing's the matter with it. Nothing at all."

He sighs. "I didn't say anything was the *matter* with it. It just looks like you spilled something on it."

"Oh, uh . . . hot chocolate! That's right, that's what it is, just hot chocolate," I say nervously, hoping I'm not overplaying it. "At breakfast. It spilled on my hand. I forgot about it. That's all. It's nothing."

He turns to me with a look of sick disgust. "Fine, it's nothing. You can shut up about it now. I wish I'd never said . . ." He notices the way I'm holding my hands behind my back. "*Now* what's the matter with you? What are you hiding? Let me see your hand again." He steps toward me.

I back away, holding my hands behind me. "What are you making such a big deal about?" I say shrilly. "Just go look out the window. Leave me alone."

He rushes toward me. On purpose, I crash into the table. He grabs my hand roughly and pulls it around in front of me to study it. For the first time, I get a good look at the back of his right hand. "Oh," I say, looking down at it, not faking now, not hiding my real reaction. "You have one too."

110

The mark on his hand is bigger than Duplicate A's, two inches across. I'm glad I risked making mine as large as I did, almost covering the entire back of my hand; I want mine to be the worst.

Duplicate B stares down at his hand, his mouth dropping open. Then he lifts his head slowly to look me in the face. "What is this?" he says softly.

"Nothing! It's nothing! I don't know what it is. Why do you think I—"

"You're hiding something. Tell me!" he snarls, and slaps me across the face.

I spin away from him, putting my hand up to my cheek, bending over so he'll get a good look at the back of my neck.

"Your neck," he whispers. He grabs my shoulders and shakes me. "Tell me! Tell me everything you know!" He hits me hard on the side of my head.

"Go to hell!" I shout, pulling away.

He pushes me down onto the bed, then leans over me, grabbing my arms. *"Tell me!"*

"The fish," I say, breathing hard. "Just like on the fish. Didn't you . . . see them?"

"I haven't been home since Monday morning." He sounds scared now. "Tell me!" He slaps me again. "I'll keep hitting you until you tell me everything you know!"

"Okay, okay." I squirm away from him, pressing myself against the wall behind the bed. "Yesterday morning, before I came here, I noticed . . . one of the fish had black marks on its right fin and the back of its head." I talk slowly, trying to catch my breath. "I didn't know what it meant, if it was the duplicate or the original. But it was acting crazy, banging its head against the aquarium. Then,

111

last night, the marks were bigger, a lot bigger. And the other fish . . . was starting to get them too." It's the story I've planned out while I've been here with him today, with no chance to think it through carefully. I'm not sure how much sense it makes. I can only hope he'll buy it. "Then, this morning, the fish with the bigger marks, the fish who got them first and went crazy . . . was dead. And the other one . . ."

"Go on! What about the other one?"

"The . . . the marks were gone," I whisper. "The fish seemed . . . to be okay."

He lets go of my arms, backs away from me and sinks into a chair. He looks at his hand again, almost in disbelief, then turns his eyes on me. "I don't get it," he says. "What do you think it means?"

"I'm not sure," I say, shaking my head.

"But which is the original and which is the duplicate?"

"I don't know. There's no way to tell. But I don't think that's the . . . the important thing about the marks."

"Then what *is* the important thing?" he says sarcastically, as though he's doubting the whole story.

"The marks kill. Once they get big enough, whoever has them will die. But when there's only one individual left, if it's not too late, they go away. That's what happened to the fish. Only one can survive." Of course, what I'm telling him is a lie. The fish with the markings did not die; the other one did. But I want him to believe that the markings are dangerous; it's my only chance of survival.

"Does the other one have them?" he asks me, trying to sound casual about it.

I nod. "I checked him out this morning. They're smaller than yours."

"Smaller?" he says, frowning.

I nod. "And mine are . . . the biggest." I close my eyes. What I'm about to say is the crux of the whole thing; if he doesn't believe this, my plan will never work. "I . . . I think it's too late for me, already. Mine are so big. And I've been feeling funny, sick, like I have a fever. And weak and dizzy. I don't think there's any way to stop it on me now. I can just tell somehow. But you, you and the other one . . ."

"His are smaller?" He kneels in front of me and reaches to grab my arm again. Then he thinks better of it, and pulls his hand away. "They're smaller? Sure you're not just trying to scare me?"

"They're smaller," I say. "But they'll keep getting bigger, on both of you, as long as you're both around." I look hard at him, speaking slowly. "The only way one of you can survive is to get rid of the other one, before it's too late. Otherwise, they'll just keep growing."

"Yeah?" he says, cocking one eyebrow at me and sitting down comfortably. "Very clever little story. Very *convenient* for you. You're going to die anyway, so we leave you alone and concentrate on each other, right? But what proof do I have that it's true?"

"The marks," I say, really feeling sick now. He's not buying it! "There they are, on both of us! You can see them. Doesn't that prove it?"

"It doesn't prove anything about what really happened to the fish. You could be making that part up. But maybe the other one saw the fish today. Where is he, anyway?"

Duplicate B gets up and goes to the window. He looks out, and then makes a sharp noise of surprise. He turns toward me. "Angela," he says.

I jump to my feet. "Angela? He brought Angela with him?" I remember, with a terrible pang, that Duplicate A said he might bring her here after school.

"No, he didn't bring her with him." Duplicate B smiles. "She's alone."

"No!" I scream, rushing at him. "Don't do it! Don't hurt her. Don't you even *touch*—"

He punches me hard on the chin, knocking me to the floor. I'm too stunned to get up for a moment. In that moment, he bends down, reaches under the bed, and pulls out a solid, three-foot length of lumber.

I struggle to my knees. "Don't hurt her! You *can't*! Please leave her alone! *Please*!"

"What difference does it make to you? If you're telling the truth, you're dead already. And if you're lying, you'll be dead soon enough anyway." He laughs, and the piece of wood swings toward me.

I hear a loud crack, and feel a terrible ringing pain on the left side of my head. Fireworks blossom, and blackness swallows them.

14

My father has turned into a thing like an octopus. He slithers juicily behind me, gaining on me. The glass wall of the laboratory bursts apart with a crash.

I open my eyes, then immediately squeeze them shut. The light is dim in here, wherever I am, but it still hurts. I lapse back into unconsciousness.

Some time later—a minute or an hour—a brighter light stings my closed eyelids. I groan, and try to turn away from it. But I can't move. My eyes blink open. A vague, blurred face won't come into focus behind the painful circle of light. I begin to remember. "Ohhh . . . turn that thing off," I mumble. "You have to hit me so hard?"

The light swings away, but it remains greenly behind my eyes, fading slowly. "It wasn't me. It was the other one," the figure says.

Maybe it's the truth. "Let me see. Shine the light on your face."

The face brightens for a moment, a rounder face than

Duplicate B's, with slightly darker hair. The light clicks off. "Oh, it *is* you," I say, feeling relieved. I struggle to move again, beginning to be aware of the tight, constricting ache in my limbs. I can't move. I must be tied up. Suddenly I'm angry. "Come on, hurry up, get me out of here!" I say, jerking my body up and down on the cement floor. "That other one's crazy; he's a monster! God, how could you be *stupid* enough to make another one?"

Duplicate A starts to move toward me, then stops. "Now do you believe I didn't put the cement block there?" he asks me.

The question infuriates me. "Sure, maybe you didn't put it there. You just created another duplicate to do it for you. Come on, untie me! What are you waiting for?"

"Tell me what happened first. And where's the other one? I want to trust you, but I have to be sure."

"Trust me, trust me! You don't know how uncomfortable this is. I won't try anything; my head hurts too much for me to even stand up. And how should I know where the other one is? The last time I saw him he was knocking me out."

But he still doesn't move. "Just tell me what happened. I have to think for a minute."

"You're a real bastard, not warning me about him, you know that? How could you just let me walk in here, knowing he was waiting for me?"

"*You* wouldn't have warned *me*."

"I never would have made another duplicate in the first place. I'm not that dumb!" I shout, struggling against the ropes again. But they're too tight, and I stop for awhile,

116

letting my head sink down onto the gritty floor. "Where are we?"

"The empty room next to the bedroom. Tell me what happened."

A little more alert now, I notice that his voice is weak and strained, as though he has a sore throat. He's not going to untie me until I talk. And I know there's something important I have to tell him, some story, but I'm still too fuzzy headed to remember what it is. I have to be careful not to say the wrong thing. But I don't see why I shouldn't tell him what happened this morning. "Okay, okay, I came straight over here when you went to school. I was expecting something else like the concrete block, so I was real careful. When I got up to the bedroom, there was—"

"Wait a minute. How'd you get past the trap on the stairs?"

"It wasn't there. We set it up later. I didn't want to, but he made me help him. How did *you* get past it?"

"He set that trap up . . . just for me?" the duplicate says.

"Sure."

"But I thought . . ." Duplicate A's voice falters.

"You thought you were safe from him? You *trusted* him?" I can hardly believe it. How can he be so naive? "Listen, that guy is a maniac. He's completely sadistic. He doesn't care about anything but himself. You didn't *know* that?"

"I . . . Oh, I don't know, I don't know."

"Your pitiful act is so phony it's *sickening*!" I lift my head and spit the words at him. "You actually worked the whole thing out *together*. You sent me here hoping he'd kill me. You're just as bad as he is!"

"No, no, he made me," Duplicate A whimpers, his voice cracking. "It's the truth. *He* wanted you to come here today. He said he'd turn against me, be my enemy, unless I went to school and you came here. But I didn't want you to."

"Why didn't you just tell me about him?"

"I told you not to come to the tower today. I told you to wait somewhere else until I came home from school and we'd go together. Remember? That . . . that was as much as I could do."

He did suggest that I stay away from the tower this morning. And he did seem very reluctant about asking me to let him go to school. It's probably true that Duplicate B forced him to do it—just as he forced me to help him make the trap today. But I still don't think I can trust Duplicate A. I'm so tired.

I take a deep breath and close my eyes. I remember the noise I heard in my dream. It must have been the ladder falling. "So how did you get past the ladder?" I ask him.

"I guess . . . I was just lucky. The concrete block fell behind me. And the ladder didn't land right on my head, it just kind of slid down on me. It hit me on the chin and it hurt my leg, but I curled up and kept my hands over my head and tried to roll with it. It knocked my breath out, but I don't think it broke anything. I do feel kind of dizzy, kind of sick. But I felt that way already."

Then I remember. The fish. The black marks. My plan—to convince both duplicates that I'm dying, no threat, but that they must kill each other off or die—comes back to me.

Duplicate B didn't believe my story—at least not then. But if I can convince Duplicate A, I might still have a chance. "Yeah, I feel pretty dizzy and sick too, and real disoriented," I say, since I want him to think the marks have progressed farther on me, and I'm starting to go crazy. But I don't say anything else yet; first I need to find out how much he knows. "So, what else do you want me to tell you before you'll untie me? My hands and feet are getting numb."

He looks away from me. "What happened when you got here? What did he do? What did he say?"

"You guys sure messed up that bedroom I cleaned. But I guess that was *his* fault, like everything else, right? I bet he hogged most of the food you paid for, didn't he. That's why you were so hungry this morning. I hope you had a nice *lunch*. Anyway, he didn't attack me or anything, for some reason. I knew right away he wasn't you, since he looks a little different."

"So he really does look different?" Duplicate A sounds relieved. "It's not just in my head?"

"He looks different. And he sure acts different. I don't know what it means about the Spee-Dee-Dupe. Maybe we'll never know. I just know he's a maniac. He tried to get me to side with him against you. And don't get upset again; it's important for you to know what he's like. He must have asked you to side with him against me, right?"

"Right," admits Duplicate A. "He said he and I were closer because our bifurcation was more recent and we had more shared experiences. He made that drawing. He said we were like brothers and you were like a distant cousin or something."

"And you lapped it all up."

119

"Try to understand," he pleads with me. "The whole reason I bifurcated again was because I was scared. I didn't trust you, and I wanted somebody on my side. Now I know it was a stupid mistake. We just have to try to deal with him."

"Well there's not much I can do tied up like this! What else do I have to tell you?"

"Just tell me everything that happened. I've got to be sure I can trust you. You can't blame me for that."

I try to give him the most important information as quickly as I can. He listens quietly, until I begin to tell him what Duplicate B said about Angela and what happened at her house on Sunday night.

"No! It wasn't like that at all," he interrupts me.

"It wasn't?" I say, lifting my head again. "She didn't call up Carl? She didn't act bored, like she was just using you to do her math problems?"

"No. Carl called *her*. And afterward she said she was tired of the way he was always checking up on her. And she wasn't bored at all. She was real friendly."

"How friendly? Did you make out with her?"

He looks away.

"Look, I kissed her yesterday, on the beach and when I took her home. Okay? So why can't you tell me if you made out with her on Sunday?"

"Well, we did make out, a little," he confesses, looking back at me. "Not much, because of her brother being there. But she didn't seem bored—not bored at all."

I can't help an agonizing rush of jealousy. And I can't keep from asking him, "What happened with her in school today?"

120

"Not much," he says, and sighs. "First of all, I felt so tired and peculiar. And I knew you'd been with her all day yesterday, so I was afraid of saying the wrong thing."

He might be telling the truth. "That's probably why she came out here after school," I say, thinking aloud. "She must have been looking for me—you, whoever— to see if anything was wrong."

He kneels quickly down beside me. "She came here? When? Where is she now?"

"I don't know. That's when he knocked me out, as soon as he saw her out the window. She must be with him."

"No!" Duplicate A gets up and starts pacing, chewing on his nails. "What's he going to do? He hates her!"

"That's for sure. And I don't get it. You and I both like her so much. Doesn't that prove you can't trust him? If you untie me, we can both try to help her."

"But do you think he might be hurting her? Do you think he really would? He said the concrete block was meant for her."

"I know." I'm dying to chew my nails too, but my hands are tied behind my back. "Maybe he's hurting her. But that would be too dangerous. It's more likely that he's just being vicious, trying to scare her away from us for good."

"I'd like to kill him!" says Duplicate A, clenching his fists. "I should have come here right after school, instead of going home first. Then I could have gotten her away from here before he saw her."

"Why did you go home first?" I ask him, wondering if it could possibly have anything to do with the fish.

"Oh, I wanted to make an appearance for a little while, so Mom wouldn't worry," he says absently.

I wonder if I should ask him about the fish. What can I lose? If he's seen them, it's already too late; he'll know that the marked fish is alive, and the unmarked fish is dead, and my plan will never work. If he hasn't seen them, I still might have a chance. "Did you happen to . . . check on the fish while you were there?"

"The fish?" he says, not paying attention. "What are we going to do about Angela?"

It's possible that he didn't see them. Maybe I'm in luck. If I can convince him, we both might be able to convince Duplicate B. But I still have to be careful. I try to remember when I first noticed the marks. I think it was yesterday morning, meaning he could have seen them before going to school. "You didn't notice, yesterday morning? The fish with the black marks in the aquarium?"

"Oh, I guess so. And then today . . ." But he's not interested in the fish. "Maybe they're outside now," he says, hurrying for the window.

"Listen to me," I say. "This is important. The black marks mean—"

He makes a startled sound. He's behind me now and I can't roll over and look at him. "What's the matter? What happened?" I ask him.

"Duplicate B, and Angela." He clears his throat, but his voice remains hoarse. "I can't believe it. Down on the beach. Hugging and kissing. Making out like crazy."

"*What?* But he hates her!"

"He sure isn't acting like it now."

I grunt, pushing furiously against the ropes. "He only *told* us he hates her, the liar! He must have had some reason for it, some little scheme. You can't trust him about *anything*! Come on, untie me so we can stop him!"

Duplicate A runs from the window, but not to untie me. He pauses in the doorway. "He knows you're tied up here, helpless," he says. "And he doesn't know I'm here. So maybe we can—"

"He'll know you're here as soon as he comes inside and sees the ladder. And I bet he *will* bring her inside. He said he wished I'd brought her in yesterday."

Duplicate A runs back to the window. "He's asking her something; he's pointing back here," he says. "He's kissing her neck."

"Hurry! Put the ladder back. Set up the trap just like it was before. Then he'll think you're not here. Then maybe we can surprise him. Jump him or something, when he's not expecting it."

"You're right!" He hurries back to the door, but suddenly stops. "Except, what'll he do if he finds out, if he catches us trying to trick him?" He groans, pressing his fists against his face. "He may do something to Angela before we can stop him. It'll be safer if I just go out there and he sees me. Then he'll have to leave her alone."

"No, you can't let him see you!" I plead with him. "He said he wanted to bring Angela here and *kill* her! We have to trick him, get him when he thinks he's safe. Put the ladder back!"

"Kill her? Angela?" he wails, and rushes out the door. He seems so frantic now that he really might be stupid enough to run outside. Even if he does try to put the ladder back, he probably won't have time to finish before they come in.

And I still haven't told him about the fish, and the marks. Does he even know he has them?

Duplicate A does not run outside. I lie there listening to the bump and scrape of the ladder as he drags it laboriously up the steps. The process goes on and on so slowly, and there's nothing I can do to help, to speed him up. And then he will have to balance it carefully, and go back for the concrete block, and make a new pool of oil, and fix the drawing of the skull. He'll never finish in time. They're probably on their way up the rocky hill right this minute.

I can't stand it. Again I struggle against the ropes. But it's useless, and only tires me and makes my head feel worse. All I can do is wriggle my fingers and toes, trying to prevent my limbs from going completely numb, doing my best not to think, not to picture Duplicate A's every movement. He's going so sluggishly it's like a slow motion replay.

He has even more trouble on the second floor landing, cursing to himself. "Balance it on the railing and the back of that chair!" I yell at him. "Then put the concrete block right on—" But my voice bounces back and forth so loudly on the bare cement walls that I choke it back. They mustn't hear me. I can't even give him instructions. He'll never make it.

Finally, he hurries down the stairs again, the ladder apparently balanced. Another eternity passes as he lugs up the concrete block. But something seems to be delaying Duplicate B. He could be having trouble convincing Angela to come inside; she's not dumb. And she must know about what happened in this place years ago. I begin to hope again. Maybe Duplicate A will finish in time.

I hear him rushing up to the third floor. He peeks in to check on me. "I'm going to go up and hide on the—"

"Go back and make a new puddle of oil. Fix the drawing!" I whisper.

"But they'll be here any second!"

"Fix it! It has to be perfect, or he'll know you're here. The oil's in the bedroom. Get going!"

He sighs, but hurries into the bedroom and back down the stairs. I squeeze my eyes shut, not wanting to think, not wanting to hear Duplicate B come in and find him.

When the door finally opens downstairs, Duplicate A is on his way up to the fourth floor, doing a good job of moving quietly. Duplicate B doesn't have to be quiet. He pounds up the stairs two at a time. Angela doesn't seem to be with him. Of course—he has to make her wait outside while he does something to me so that I won't make any noise. Will he hit me again, to make sure I'm unconscious? Will he do something worse? All I can do is pretend I'm still knocked out, and hope.

But he doesn't come up immediately. I listen to him

move the cement block and take the ladder off the railing on the second floor landing. He's dismantling the trap—thank God he's not going to use it on Angela. Finally he rushes up to the third floor. I brace myself, doing my best to play dead. But he only comes as close as the bedroom, next door to me, and then rushes back downstairs. He must have gotten a towel to wipe up the puddle of oil. I breathe deeply, grateful for a little more time. But in less than a minute, he's on his way up again—up to me.

I keep my eyes closed, hoping I'm in approximately the same position as when he left me. He stops in the bedroom again—to get the piece of lumber?—and then he's in the room, standing above me, panting.

Downstairs the door squeals open. "Hey, where are you? It's dark in here," Angela calls out.

"Just wait right there. I'll be down in a second with the light," shouts Duplicate B.

"But what are you doing?"

"Making it *nice* for you. Almost ready now." He pokes his foot into my ribs, pushing me back and forth. I'm tense with dread, expecting him to hit me with the wood again, but I try to make my body limp, rolling as he prods me.

He takes his foot away and comes closer, squatting down. His breath smells medicinal and rotten. The flashlight goes on, an inch away from my eyes. I feel his thumb and finger on my eyelid, pulling it up, and I let it go, not resisting. I'm still trying not to go rigid, fighting the natural impulse to steel myself against the expected blow.

The flashlight moves away. Have I passed the eye test? He pulls my head up suddenly by the hair, then lets it go. I tighten my neck, but only for an instant; I quickly let my head thud down onto the floor with teeth-jarring impact, hoping he didn't notice the delay.

"David! I'm getting tired of waiting!"

I long to call out to Angela, to tell her to run, get away before it's too late. But I don't. She probably wouldn't run away; it would only make her more curious.

"Just be patient; it'll be worth the wait!" Duplicate B calls back, doing his best to sound cheerful. But there is a frantic edge to his voice. He lifts my head again, roughly. I doubt that I'm capable of letting it bang down on the floor that hard another time. But he doesn't drop it immediately. He works something soft and greasy around the back of my neck first, which cushions the blow when he does let go of my hair. Then his hand is on my chin and just in time I relax my jaw. He pulls my mouth open and jams something into it, something that can only be a pair of socks—a pair of very dirty socks, judging by the taste and the smell. I congratulate myself on how well I manage to stifle my gag reflex. He twists the towel which he has pulled around the back of my head, and knots it several times, very tightly, and shoves the knot into my mouth on top of the socks. It is the towel which he has just used to wipe up the lamp oil, and my throat constricts, I gag, there is no way of controlling it. But he finally stands up; at least he's not going to hit me again.

When the blow does come, it is so unexpected that I am not braced against it at all.

But this time I don't stay out for as long; I must be building up a tolerance to being knocked on the head. When I begin to be aware of sounds again, Angela and

Duplicate B seem to be still on their way up. "Just wait right here. I'll be back in a second," Duplicate B says. I can hardly hear him above the ringing in my ears. It's difficult to breathe with the socks and the towel filling my mouth; I have to snort through my nose.

"Where are you going *now*?"

"I've got to fix the door so nobody else can come in," he says, on his way down.

"Well, hurry up, okay? I'm getting tired of standing around and waiting for you."

He's doing something to prevent Duplicate A from coming in and interrupting whatever he plans to do with Angela. At least that means he believes that Duplicate A isn't here. But what's he going to do to the door? He's probably rigging up another trap there, now that Angela is inside. I'll have to try to remember that, if I need to make a quick exit later.

"Where do those stairs go?" Angela says, when he finally comes back. The dizziness and the brutal pain in my head have subsided slightly; I am alert enough now to tell that her voice is coming from the third floor landing.

"The observation room. Want to take a look?"

I remember that Duplicate A is up in the observation room. There is no place to hide there, no closets, no little rooms.

"Sure, let's go up," Angela says.

"You have beautiful hair," says Duplicate B.

If they go upstairs now, we won't be able to take Duplicate B by surprise. There goes that hope.

"Come on. What are you waiting for?" Angela says.

"Oh, we can go up there later," Duplicate B says casually. He's impatient to get her into the bedroom. "First

I want to show you the room I cleaned up and made nice just for you."

"Just for *me*? How thoughtful of you," she says with some sarcasm, but she goes along with him. Now I can relax a little about Duplicate A. But I can't relax about trying to breathe. My mouth is filling with saliva. Every time I try to swallow, I get a powerful taste of dirty socks and lamp oil. I try to keep my gagging as quiet as possible.

Angela and Duplicate B talk about the room for a few minutes. I can hear them pretty well, since there is only one thin wall between us. He asks her to sit down and get comfortable. I hear the bedsprings creak. Then Angela begins to giggle.

I remember kissing her yesterday, and how wonderful it was. That's what Duplicate B must be experiencing right this minute. I don't want to picture what's going on in there, but I can't help it; the images of the two of them together force their way into my mind. Duplicate B is better looking than me, with his great complexion and curlier hair.

Jealousy eats at me. I'm raging inside. I can't stand it. I have to stop them. But what can I do? I can't move, I can't make any noise, I can't breathe without gagging. It all depends on Duplicate A. He must be able to tell what's happening, listening from upstairs. Maybe jealousy will prompt him to take action.

I don't believe in ESP, but there is still a possibility that he will think of the same plan that is forming in my mind. He's got to get downstairs and past the bedroom door without being noticed. Then he can untie me. And the two of us can attack Duplicate B while he's distracted with Angela, off his guard, at his most vulnerable. If we can manage to get him tied up, then we will be in control.

Angela is still giggling, but there's an uncomfortable sound to it. "Hey, David, wait a minute. Don't . . . You weren't like this yesterday."

"What's the matter?" Duplicate B says in a husky voice. "Don't you like me?"

"Sure. A lot. I just want to . . . get to know you a little better, before . . ."

"But that's what we're *doing,* Angela . . . mmh . . . getting to know each other better. . . ."

I never knew I was capable of hating anyone as much as I now hate Duplicate B. I can't wait to get in there and pull him away from her. So get down here Duplicate A and untie me!

I'm lying with my head facing the corridor, which is dimly lit by the afternoon sun coming through a narrow window at the far end. A shadow moves in the patch of sunlight; I hear the scrape of a footstep on the gritty floor.

"What was that? I heard something," Angela says, looking for an excuse to distract Duplicate B.

The shadow freezes.

"Oh, come on, relax. I didn't hear anything."

"It sounded like . . . like a footstep."

"There's nobody else here, Angie," Duplicate B says, with a soft chuckle. "And if anybody comes in down-stairs, we'll hear it, loud and clear. Loosen up, don't be so stiff, enjoy yourself. Isn't this nice, being so cozy here with me?"

"Yeah, but just . . ."

"Mmmh," says Duplicate B, and the sleeping bag rustles on the bed.

The shadow moves in the corridor. Duplicate A steps through the door. I lift my head, with difficulty. He kneels beside me, his finger to his lips, and I nod as well as I can. Right away, he starts on the towel. I strain to keep my head lifted to make it as easy for him as I can. I see the concern on his face as he works. Unlike Duplicate B, he does have some human feelings. I might be able to trust him after all.

He pulls off the towel and sets it silently on the floor, then gingerly reaches into my mouth and extracts the socks, which are dripping with my saliva. I throw back my head and take a deep breath, as quietly as I can. He waits a moment, then gently rolls me over and begins on the rope around my hands.

It takes a long time; Duplicate B did a thorough job. As he works, we are both aware of the noises coming from the next room—Angela continuing to resist, Duplicate B making wet sounds and ignoring her protests.

Duplicate A gets my left hand free and begins on the right hand, which is attached to my bound feet by several lengths of rope. He must be noticing the mark now. What will he make of it? And how can I tell him about it if we can't talk?

Finally, after what seems like an hour, the last knot is untied. I roll over on my back, stretching. It hurts, but we don't have much time, and I have to get my limbs ready to move soon. I try to ignore the pain, rubbing my arms and legs, flexing my feet, stretching again. At last

132

I manage to sit up, my muscles aching. Duplicate A watches me, grimacing sympathetically. I hold the back of my right hand up to his face.

He nods, indicating he has noticed the triangular mark, and then shrugs to tell me he doesn't know what it means. He bites his lip, making a hopeless gesture. He wants to communicate, but doesn't know how we can.

I pull the pen out of my shirt pocket, my fingers so stiff I can barely grasp it. I get to my knees, as quietly as possible, and take from my pants pocket the piece of paper on which I had planned to practice painting the marks but never had time. *Look at your right hand,* I write on the paper, barely legibly, and pass it to him.

He reads it, then shakes his head at me, frowning, not understanding. I point furiously at his right hand. And finally he glances at it. His mouth drops open. He really hasn't noticed it until now.

I gesture at him to give me the paper. He looks slowly up at me. I think for a moment, not sure what to say next. I still don't know if he ever noticed the marks on the fish. I'm taking a big risk now. If he saw the marked fish today, and it was alive, he'll know I'm lying to him. I'll lose his trust; he won't want to side with me against Duplicate B. It might not be worth it. Duplicate B doesn't believe me about the fish. Maybe I should just give up on this plan.

But if I *can* convince Duplicate A, then we might both be able to convince Duplicate B. And then they really will leave me alone. Duplicate A seemed so vague about the fish earlier. Maybe he didn't see it today. Maybe the risk is worth it. I write, my hand moving more easily now:

I saw same mark on fish. Kills. Too late for me now. Will kill both of you—unless get rid of him first. I pass him the piece of paper.

He reads it. He looks at me and shakes his head miserably. It's almost as though he's saying he doesn't want me to give up yet, doesn't want me to die. Does that mean he believes me?

He reaches out for the pen, and I hand it to him. He writes something and gives me back the paper. I read it. And in that one moment, everything changes.

On it he has written, in my handwriting: *Saw dead fish with marks in tank today. Now I understand.*

16

I grab the pen, excited now, wanting to question him, to make doubly sure the fish with the marks really did die. But I stop myself in time. It's not supposed to be a surprise to me. I quickly drop the pen and nod, closing my eyes and trying to look miserable.

It's not easy, because my first reaction is joy. I can hardly believe my luck. Now I know what the marks really mean. The marked fish must have killed the original fish, and then died itself in some kind of automatic process that's intrinsic to being a duplicate. Both the duplicates are marked, and I'm not. They will die automatically. That means I have a chance!

But not a very big chance, I quickly realize. I have to survive through the period of murderous insanity they will both be entering at any time. And how long will that period last, before the marks kill them?

Duplicate A reaches out and gently touches my cheek. It's not an act. He believes I'm going to die, and he feels sorry for me. And here I am, lying to him, rejoicing at the fact that he is doomed.

But what choice do I have? There's nothing I can do to save him. And Duplicate A's news means that if I hold out long enough, I'll survive.

I can't control my emotions any longer. My throat constricts. Tears of relief spill out of my eyes.

Duplicate A writes again, and hands me the paper. *You mean the* presence *of a duplicate creates the marks? But why?*

I think carefully before answering. I have to keep both stories straight in my mind—the one I'm telling them, and the truth. And I *do* feel guilty as I write out the lie: *Duplicates short-lived. Spreads to original too. Tested it with fish. Only way to stop it is to get rid of all but one individual— him or you. Then marks will go away.*

Duplicate A lifts his eyes from the note and looks toward the bedroom. "Please wait, David, *please*," Angela is begging. "I have to go to the bathroom."

"No, you don't," Duplicate B tells her. "Come on, doll. Just relax."

Duplicate A is chewing his lip. He's beginning to understand how vulnerable he is. According to my story, he is the only obstacle to Duplicate B's survival. *Does he know about the marks?* Duplicate A writes on the piece of paper.

What do I tell him now? In the context of my story, if I'm on his side I should have kept the information about the fish from Duplicate B. That would be the way to protect Duplicate A, so that Duplicate B will *not* think he has to kill him soon in order to survive. But if *I'm* going to survive, they both have to believe the story. And I've already told Duplicate B. How can I explain this betrayal to Duplicate A? What excuse do I have?

I look away from him, squeezing my hands together. I look back and mouth the words, "I'm sorry."

His expression changes instantly, his face hardening. He thrusts his fist at me. He has every right to be furious. And how soon is his mind going to go, anyway? My only recourse is to appeal to the compassion he felt only a minute ago. I gesture toward the piece of wood, which is lying on the floor beside him, then scribble, *Couldn't help it! He saw marks. Hit me until I told. But he didn't believe me. Have to get him and tie him up now, while we can.*

He reads the note; his breathing quickens.

"That's right, Angie. Relax, relax, honey. Ohhh, you're so nice. . . ." Duplicate B soothes her in a disgustingly throaty, intimate voice.

Duplicate A sits up quickly, his head swivelling toward the bedroom. I hope his rage is focussing away from me, onto Duplicate B. He grabs the rope and shoves it at me abruptly. He picks up the piece of wood and stands up, staggering a little. I get slowly to my feet, my muscles screaming. I make a sloppy coil out of the rope, leaving several feet free at the end. I hold the coil in my left hand, the loose end in my right. I nod at him. We move quietly out into the corridor.

"You're so beautiful, Angie. Did anybody ever tell you that before?" Duplicate B is murmuring. I slip to the other side of the doorway, and we both peek into the bedroom.

"Yeah, somebody told me that before—*you* did, yesterday," Angela says, her voice a little shrill. "Your memory is really lousy, David, you know that? You were like a different person yesterday, nicer, not so pushy."

They're both stretched out on the bed. We're in luck: Angela has her back to the wall, Duplicate B has his back to us. If we move fast enough, we might be able to get to him before her reaction gives us away. But still we hesitate.

"Aw, I'm still nice, Angie," Duplicate B coos at her, as though he's talking to a pet. "I just like you better now because I know you better. I care about you more than anybody. Don't you care about me at all?" He props himself up on one elbow, looking down at her, blocking her view of the doorway.

I glance for a second at Duplicate A. This is our chance, while she can't see us. What are we waiting for?

"Sure, I care about you, David. But what's the—"

"Then prove it!" Duplicate B throws himself on top of her. We rush into the room.

"David! Stop it this minute or I'll scream!" Then Angela, struggling, looks past his ear and sees us. She screams.

A swings the piece of wood at B's head. But B has already begun to turn around. He sees it coming and tries to duck out of the way. And A doesn't hit him hard enough. He just doesn't have it in him to be that brutal— they really are different. The wood strikes Duplicate B's shoulder and clatters to the floor.

Angela, scrambling off the bed, is screaming words at us now—she has seen what we look like. "No! I don't believe . . . What *are* you?"

I'm trying to get the rope around him. But my muscles are stiff, I'm clumsy, and B moves fast. Then A manages to pin B's arms behind his back. I struggle with the rope, looping it once around his hands, twice, beginning to pull it tight.

Suddenly A lets go, jerking backward. Angela has him by the hair. "Stop it!" he tries to tell her. "Let go! You don't understand!"

"Leave him alone!" she shouts.

Duplicate B kicks A hard in the stomach, and he crumples up, pulled backwards by Angela. The rope is tangled now. B pulls his hands free and lurches away from the bed. I try to get the rope around his knees as he jerks and thrashes, not paying attention to his arms. The wood slams against my head a third time, an impossible pain. I hit the floor, knocking the table over. Soft drink cans rain down on my face. I'm semi-conscious, but too stunned to move.

"Stop it, Angela! Let go of me! *He's* the bad one!" I hear Duplicate A shouting in the distance.

"Yeah. Let go of him, Angela," comes Duplicate B's voice. My vision is blurred, the room is spinning, but I can just see him standing commandingly by the bed, brandishing the piece of wood. "Quick, come over here and get the rope. Tie up the other one while he's out."

"But . . . but, who *are* they?" Angela wants to know. "How can they . . . look like they're you?"

"Come over here and get the rope!" Duplicate B orders her.

Duplicate A kneels beside me, to see how I am, to protect me, to keep her away. And that's when Duplicate B gets his arm tight around Angela's neck, pulling her against him, holding the piece of wood with his other hand. She

139

makes a choking sound. He's squeezing her neck so tightly she can't even scream.

"*You* tie him up, or I'll smash her teeth in!" Duplicate B snarls at A.

A rushes at him, but he holds Angela to the side and kicks him again, in the groin. Duplicate A staggers away. He seems too weak now, probably because of the marks, to put up a fight. And I'm too dizzy and dazed from being hit on the head three times and tied up for so long to do anything but lie there feeling sick. I also haven't had much sleep for days.

I wonder, briefly, why Duplicate A seems so much more weakened by the marks than Duplicate B, since B's are bigger. Maybe it's that Duplicate A, being both the duplicate of me and the original of Duplicate B, is more fragile, more vulnerable.

But he's still making an attempt at resistance. "You can't . . . make me tie him up," Duplicate A says, his voice cracking.

"Her pretty smile will never be the same again," Duplicate B tells him. "You know I'll do it. Tie him *now*. Start with the feet."

He ties my feet, then my hands, but not tight. I can't tell if I'll be able to get out of it or not, whenever I might recover from the blows on the head. B seems to be whispering something to Angela. But he doesn't release her until Duplicate A finishes with me and gets up and backs away.

"Sorry, Angie doll," Duplicate B says immediately, "But there was no other way I—"

She's backing away from him. "I'll kill you if you ever

get near me again," she says, sounding as though she means it. "How could you *do* that?"

"Oh, Angie, you know I could never really hurt you. But threatening it was the only way," he explains, doing a brilliant acting job. "I had to get him to tie that one up. They want to kill me. And they would have. They're maniacs, monsters. You have to believe me."

"No, no, *he's* the monster!" says Duplicate A, his voice pitifully hoarse. "Neither of us would have done that to you. And I'll get him for it, I swear I will!" He picks up the lantern from the table, raising it like a weapon.

"See? See how violent and brutal he is?" says Duplicate B, chuckling.

Angela backs toward the door, shaking her head. "I'm getting out of here. This is crazy. I can't . . . can't understand any of it." But she doesn't leave. Frightened as she is, she's just too curious. "Except . . . who are they? What's going on here?"

"Don't worry about that," says Duplicate B. "Just go. Get away, before the crazy one with the lantern attacks *you*. And don't say a thing to anybody. I'll explain it all later."

"No!" says Duplicate A, his voice firmer. "You just don't want her to see what you're going to do. And she deserves to know. She's part of it now."

"He's right," I manage to say, my head finally beginning to clear. "Tell her everything."

"Who asked you?" says Duplicate B, kicking me in the ribs.

"How can you *do* that to him? He's sick. He's . . . he's dying," says Duplicate A, his voice breaking.

141

"You mean you fell for that stupid story? Can't you see it's just—"

"Stop arguing and tell me what's going *on*!" Angela shrieks.

"They're duplicates," A tells her, standing straighter. "I made copies of myself with this machine I found. But it wasn't like . . . I mean, it's hard to explain," he rambles, sounding confused, shaking his head. "It's just that . . . I thought it would make things easier. God, was I wrong about that. And now . . . it's all so complicated, so hard to explain."

"But what did you mean about that one being sick, dying? What's wrong with him?" she wants to know.

Now he's going to tell her about the fish. And when he says that the fish with the marks is dead, Duplicate B will finally believe my story. And then I'll be safe. They'll both leave me alone, and concentrate on each other.

"Why is he sick? Because . . . because of . . ." Duplicate A's voice falters again. "Umm . . . I don't know why. I didn't really mean to say he was dying. He's just weak, because the other one beat him up, I guess."

His mind is deteriorating; he's having trouble thinking logically. But he's not confused enough—as I hoped he would be—to tell Duplicate B about the fish. He doesn't want Duplicate B to believe my story, that he has to kill A soon in order to survive. He wants Duplicate B to think he has plenty of time.

And suddenly, so do I.

It's crazy. I'm not safe yet; I'm tied up again, more vulnerable than ever. But now I don't want my plan to work; I don't want to manipulate Duplicate A's death.

He felt compassion for me, and I can't help feeling it for him. I want to give him more time; I want to protect him. It's my stupid human decency coming out again.

And there's still a chance Duplicate B won't buy the story I made up.

"But you *did* say he was dying," Duplicate B says slowly. "And now you're denying it. You're covering something up. You're lying." He steps toward him, lifting the piece of wood. "Tell me the truth!"

"He *is* telling you the truth," I say, managing to sit up, weaving. "*I'm* the one who was lying. That . . . that whole story about the fish was a lie. It won't do you any good to kill him."

"Huh?" Both duplicates turn and stare at me.

"You were right before. I just made up that story to protect myself," I tell Duplicate B. I know it's insane, I know I'm giving up whatever safety I might have had. But I just don't want him to hurt Duplicate A. "It's *not* true that only one can survive. You don't have to kill each other. It won't make any difference."

"He's right," Duplicate A says. Now he knows what I'm doing, that I'm trying to protect him—and in a way, that makes it worth the risk. "We're telling the truth. He'll get better. We'll all get better. There's . . . lots of time, plenty of time, we just need to take it easy for—"

Duplicate B's mind is deteriorating in a different way. He's not as confused, but he's a lot more rash and violent. "Stop mumbling lies, you stupid bastard," he says. "I can see the mark on you. And you believe the story too; I can tell. About the marks, and how only one of us can survive, and it's too late for that one"—he jerks his head

143

at me—"I can tell. And you *wouldn't* believe it, unless you saw it happen to the fish yourself. So it must be true!"

"No, no, it's a lie!"

"Bull!" Duplicate B spits at him.

"I'm telling the truth!" I scream. "Can't you see why I would make up that story, so you'd leave me alone and try to kill each other? Believe me!"

But it's too late. "Shut up, both of you!" Duplicate B roars. He can't believe we're telling him the truth, because he would never tell us the truth. All we've been doing is convincing him to believe my story.

And now that Duplicate B finally does believe, his reaction is instant and unhesitating. He rushes at A with the wooden club.

Duplicate A strikes out with the lantern. The two weapons meet. The lamp shatters. Shards of glass skitter across the sandy cement floor.

Duplicate A isn't wearing shoes. He must have taken them off upstairs, so they wouldn't hear him sneaking down. He backs toward the door, stepping on glass, holding up the lamp. It's a better weapon now, jagged with broken glass. "Come near me and I'll rip your head open," he says. But he doesn't sound tough enough. For an instant he glances over at Angela. She's looking frantically back and forth between the two of them, as though she doesn't know which one to believe.

"What do you think you're going to do? Run away and hide somewhere? Then we'll *all* die, you idiot. We're settling this *now*!" Duplicate B's lips curl back from his teeth. He rushes toward him.

Duplicate A turns and runs out the door. Duplicate B

starts to follow. "Leave him alone!" Angela screams as she hurls herself at him, tackling him and pulling him to the floor and the broken glass. But she slows him only briefly. He kicks her away, scrambles to his feet, and rushes down the corridor.

I've already got my hands free; Duplicate A wisely did a lousy job of tying me up. "Quick, help me with my feet! We've got to stop him," I tell her. "Hurry!" It's not just that I want to protect Duplicate A. If Duplicate B survives this fight, the next thing he'll do is kill me too. It doesn't matter what story anybody believes any more. Duplicate B has entered the homicidal stage, and we are both his enemies.

"Help!" Duplicate A shouts from the stairs. "He's the evil one. Stop him! Save me!"

Angela is amazingly fast and efficient with the rope, given the situation and the emotional state she is in. In seconds we are both following them up the stairs. Poor Duplicate A really is confused. Why didn't he run *down*? Upstairs there is only the observation room, from which there is no escape. Duplicate B laughs above us. "Great! Stupider than I thought. Got you cornered now."

We pound into the observation room. Amazingly, unbelievably, there *is* an exit, and Duplicate A has found it. He is already at the top of a metal ladder bolted into the far wall, holding the lantern in his teeth, pushing with his head against a wooden trapdoor in the ceiling. Duplicate B, slowed by the impact of Angela's tackle, is still at the bottom of the ladder. He hesitates. He doesn't want to discard the club, but it's too big for him to hold in his mouth, and he needs both hands to climb the ladder. He tosses back his head and growls, then hurls down the club and leaps onto the ladder.

I rush across the room and throw myself onto the ladder to try to pull him back down. He kicks me in the head—in the same place—and I slip back, almost falling off. Angela pushes me from below, steadying me, saving me from falling. I tighten my grip and pull myself to the top. I climb through the trapdoor and drag myself up onto the roof.

The beach stretches out far below. It's windy today, the sun blinking on and off as cloud shadows roll across the choppy water. I look around for a moment, my head spinning, amazed at being up here so unexpectedly.

But that one moment has given Duplicate B all the time he needs. He has knocked the lantern away from Duplicate A and is facing him at the edge of the roof. There is no railing. The rocky cliff is five stories down. I move toward them quietly, carefully, so that Duplicate B won't hear me coming, and won't make any instant moves.

Duplicate A is so weak and confused now that he is swaying, barely able to keep his balance. "How can you *do* this?" he is sobbing. "How can you stand it? How will you feel afterwards?"

"I'll feel *alive,* crybaby," Duplicate B jeers at him, and with one casual thrust of his arm he pushes him off the roof.

"Don't!" I scream, too late. I freeze, a couple of yards from the edge, listening to Duplicate A's terrible wailing cry. It doesn't last very long.

It is so total, so sudden, that for a moment I can't take it in, can't move. Angela, beside me now, is panting, watching Duplicate B. He is leaning fearlessly over the edge, fascinated by what he sees below. His hands are on his knees; he seems to be laughing. I could easily push him now. But I don't.

Finally he straightens up, slowly turns around, and stretches his arms luxuriously over his head. He grins at us. "I knew you wouldn't push me," he says, pulling up the loose sweat pants. "You just don't have the nerve." He cranes his neck as he talks, twisting his head strangely, making me think of the sea gull that bifurcated so long ago. "You can't really have any respect for someone like that, can you, Angie?" he asks her. "Someone who doesn't have the courage to make a move for his own survival, who just stands there? Someone that weak and gutless hardly even *deserves* to survive, don't you think?"

Angela turns to me with a funny look on her face. She

backs away from me. Then she actually smiles—a sad, frightened smile—at Duplicate B. And she nods at him. "You're right, David," she says. "Now I know you're the real one. You're the only one who's making any sense."

Duplicate B crows with delight. "Good *girl,* Angie!"

"No, Angela! Don't!" This is the worst nightmare of all. Angela siding with a duplicate is what I've been afraid of all along. "You saw what he was like, how he hurt you. You heard what the two of us said about him. He's evil, he's a maniac!"

His smile fades. "What difference does it make what you said, or what he said? He's nothing but a squashed pile of guts now. The sea gulls will have a feast. One down, one to go." He beckons to me. "Come on, aren't you going to try to push me off? Come on, I dare you." He holds out his arms. The wind lifts his hair, golden in the sunlight; clouds drift serenely behind him.

I don't know what to say. I turn helplessly toward Angela, who's watching Duplicate B with wide, trusting eyes. He's right. I don't have the guts to push him off, even though I know how evil he is, even though he wants to kill me. I just can't do it. I know I'm an idiot, a fool. And Angela knows it too.

"Come on, do something!" Duplicate B shouts suddenly, his face reddening, still twisting his neck in that strange way. "Because in another second, you're going over the edge. And once you're gone, this mark will go too." He lifts his right hand, with its neat triangular black spot. He doesn't seem to be aware of how much his hand is trembling. "And when this goes, I'll be safe. I'll be the survivor—like I knew I would be, all along."

"Wrong," I tell him. Now the truth is my only chance.

148

"That mark will never go away, no matter what you do to me. You're dead. It'll kill you, like it killed the fish. And *this* mark—" I desperately hold out my hand to him, "—this mark is painted on. The one on my neck is too. They're fake. I made them this morning. I don't have any marks at all."

"Huh?" For a second he looks baffled, not angry. His cheek is twitching. "You painted them on? Why would you do that?"

"To make you believe my story. To make you think I was too far gone to worry about. It's the truth, I swear it is! Only the duplicates get the marks. And the marks destroy them. There's no reason to kill me. You still won't have a chance."

He screws up his face in violent disgust. "Talk all you want. Talk, talk, talk!" he shouts, his voice high-pitched and strained, his head jerking from side to side. "I'll never believe anything you say. It doesn't matter. I'm getting rid of you, just like the other one. I'm doing it now." He steps toward me.

"David, look out!" Angela suddenly screams at him, pointing. "Another duplicate, over there!"

Duplicate B jumps and turns. His foot comes down inside the smashed lamp. He tries to kick it away, crying out in pain as the broken glass cuts into his bare ankle. He lurches away from me, shaking his foot, panicked. There is no other duplicate coming. I start toward him, wondering what I'm going to do.

But before I reach him he stumbles backwards, over the edge. The sound he makes as he falls, a bellowing enraged howl, is very different from the piteous wail of Duplicate A.

18

We are sitting together on the couch at Angela's house, watching the video of *Interstellar Pig*. Angela's parents are not at home. Neither is her brother. My arm is around her. Her head is on my shoulder.

"Amazing," she whispers, glancing at the movie. "The lichen seems so *real*."

She pulls her head away and looks at me when I don't respond. "David? David, are you paying any attention to this movie at all?"

"Huh? Oh, yeah, sure, it's great."

She sighs, and returns her head to my shoulder. I pull her against me. "You've got to stop thinking about it all the time, David. You've got to at least try."

She's right. But how do you make yourself stop thinking about something that turns and turns like a repeating loop inside your head? The worst part is the sound Duplicate A made when he went off the roof. I never knew you could remember sounds so clearly. Maybe it's because I often make the same sound myself, waking up in the middle of the night from a bad dream. Mom and Dad don't understand it.

Of course Angela was extremely upset, too, at the time. We both cried a lot, when it was over, in the bedroom at the tower. Part of it was from relief. I don't know how many times I told her how amazing it was that she got Duplicate B to trust her and then startled him into falling off the roof. I still can't get over how she pulled it off in the middle of that crazy situation, how she instinctively did it.

And she told me, over and over again, not to feel so bad about Duplicate A. He was going to die anyway, it was inevitable, maybe it was even better for him to have it happen so quickly. She's probably right. But I still can't stand it that we never had a chance to settle things at the end, another chance to trust each other. It's my responsibility that he ever existed. He was my enemy, some of the time. But he was also a human being—a decent one in the end. And what happened to him was my fault.

Almost as bad as the sound of his voice when he died was the sight of their bodies, sprawled together on the rocks underneath the tower. Angela worked right along with me, covering them with rocks and branches and leaves and sand. We've only been back there once since then, but we are constantly checking the news, and no one has found them. That was three weeks ago. If they're anything like the duplicate fish, they've probably disintegrated by now.

We talked about that a lot. It's only logical that the duplicates would be short-lived. The Spee-Dee-Dupe must have been designed for short-term use, for missions only a few days long. After that, the duplicate's built-in self-destruct mechanism takes over. It has to be there, to protect society from the danger of several individuals running around all thinking they're the same person.

That protection is just about the only good thing about the device. I'll never understand why the duplicates have to go crazy, or why Duplicate B was so evil right from the beginning. They seem to get worse the farther away they are from the original. In that case, what would the duplicate of a duplicate of a duplicate of a duplicate be like? Would it be four times more monstrous than he was? Why would anyone design a machine to work that way? But maybe it wasn't designed that way. Maybe it was just malfunctioning.

In any case, we had to decide what to do with the Spee-Dee-Dupe. I would have liked to smash the thing to pieces, but I didn't dare. Who knows what is inside it? Whatever makes it work could be worse than radioactive, and breaking it open could release it.

I couldn't think of any place safe enough to bury it. All we could do was put it back in the ocean. But I wanted it deep in the ocean, so it wouldn't just get washed up again right away. The next weekend Angela and I rented a boat with a little outboard motor. We chugged around to the tower, and I ran up and got it from under the bed. Then we headed directly out.

Several miles from shore, where the boat rocked a lot and I figured it was pretty deep, we put the Spee-Dee-Dupe in ten layers of plastic bags, filled the innermost bag with rocks, knotted the ends, pushing the air out, and dropped the bundle over the edge. It sank fast. The plastic should keep it protected from any creatures, as long as the plastic lasts. Even if something eats through it, it probably won't do much harm to have defective duplicates of fish or ocean worms or plankton.

But it won't stay inside the bag forever. And ocean currents are funny things. It *could* get washed up again. A fishing trawler might pull it up in a net. And then what will happen? Who will find it? Someone who will figure out how to make duplicates, the way I did? That person wouldn't realize what would happen any more than I did. I can't stop worrying about it.

"David?" Angela whispers, moving closer.

"Yeah?"

"Does this help to distract you?" She kisses me.

"Yeah, that helps a lot," I say, a little while later. "Except, I keep wondering . . ."

"What?"

"You really didn't think Duplicate B was better looking than me?"

She sighs. "For the tenth time, yeah, sure, maybe he was, in a sort of plastic, soap opera kind of way. But nobody could stand to be around him for long. He was horrible, David. You know that. The opposite of you. And being with you . . . you know how I feel about being with you. *This* is how I feel about being with you."

"And this is how I feel about being with you," I tell her. "I think maybe I love you, Angela."

"I love hearing it, David."

At that moment, a new idea occurs to me. Does the Spee-Dee-Dupe have a memory? It probably does keep a record of the genetic material it reproduces. That means Duplicate A and Duplicate B could still be inside there, ready to come out if a certain button got pushed, accidentally or otherwise. And what would the duplicates do if they did get out?

I start to mention this to Angela. She doesn't want to talk about it. She wants to distract me again. And this time she succeeds.

Until the phone rings.